COMING NEXT TIME...

STORIES! ARTICLES!
SHERLOCK HOLMES & DR. WATSON!

Sherlock Holmes Mystery Magazine #24
is just a few months away...watch for it!

Not a subscriber yet?
Send $59.95 for 6 issues (postage paid in the U.S.) to:

Wildside Press LLC
Attn: Subscription Dept.
9710 Traville Gateway Dr. #234
Rockville MD 20850

You can also subscribe online at
www.wildsidepress.com

FROM WATSON'S NOTEBOOK

Two of Holmes's adventures appear in this issue of *Sherlock Holmes Mystery Magazine*. First is my own rendering of the slightly gruesome case of the engineer's thumb—gruesome, perhaps, to the lay reader if not the physician, though I admit the first sight of the poor chap's maimed hand gave me a bit of a turn. Secondly is David Marcum's rendering of the tragic business at Lytton House, which he chose to write in the form of a radio script with sound effects.

I also note that my friend and coeditor Mr Kaye has included two adventures of the American sleuth Nero Wolfe, who is proportioned rather like Holmes's brother Mycroft, though from what I've read Mr Wolfe is even larger. Yes, I have read many of his amanuensis's stories of their cases and enjoy them, though I've never been able to prevail upon Holmes to do the same.

And now here is Mr Kaye.

– John H Watson, M D

⚹　⚹　⚹　⚹

The contributors to this issue are predominantly those who have appeared in earlier issues: Dan Andriacco, Laird Long, an article by Gary Lovisi and a new story by Steve Liskow. Robert Lopresti's tale echoes my love for Gilbert and Sullivan. As Dr. Watson mentions above, two Nero Wolfe stories round out the issue. One of them involves a surprising "package" left on Wolfe's doorstep, while the second Wolfean case is, like David Marcum's Holmes story, a radio play. Its author is the late steering committee member of The Wolfe Pack, the society devoted to Rex Stout's West 35th Street detective. Henry was much loved by Pack members for, among other things, the Nero Wolfe quizzes he wrote for the annual Black Orchid Banquets. They were always so challenging that when he died, one of the memorials the Pack delivered was my own verse meant to be sung to the tune of Stephen Foster's "Aura Lee."

> Let's remember Henry E.
> With a lot of love.
> Where's he gone? No mystery—

SHERLOCK HOLMES
MYSTERY MAGAZINE

VOL. 7, NO. 2   **Issue #23**

FEATURES

NON FICTION

FICTION

ART & CARTOONS

STAFF

Publisher: John Betancourt
Editor: Marvin Kaye
Non-fiction Editor: Carla Coupe
Assistant Editor: Steve Coupe

Sherlock Holmes Mystery Magazine is published by Wildside Press, LLC. Single copies: $10.00 + $3.00 postage. U.S. subscriptions: $59.95 (postage paid) for the next 6 issues in the U.S.A., from: Wildside Press LLC, Subscription Dept. 9710 Traville Gateway Dr., #234; Rockville MD 20850. International subscriptions: see our web site at www.wildsidepress.com. Available as an ebook through all major ebook etailers, or our web site, www.wildsidepress.com.

He's quizzing them above.

Questions anent Sherlock Holmes
And Nero Wolfe, no doubt,
And I'll bet he's stumping
Dr. Doyle and Mr. Stout.

When they heard it, Stout's two daughters Barbara and Rebecca said if Dad was stumped, he probably never would admit it!

Canonically Yours,
Marvin Kaye

ASK MRS HUDSON

by Mrs (Martha) Hudson

Dear Mrs Hudson,

I am recently widowed and, to my surprise, suddenly very wealthy. I had no idea that my husband was so well-off! But between his will and the insurance that he took out on his own life, I am suddenly in receipt of approximately three million pounds!!!

My question is what shall I do with this huge sum? I am a woman of modest means and have no appetites or cravings that require more than a modest income for clothing, food and housing.

Perplexed,

(Mrs) Valerie Milverton

⚹　⚹　⚹

Dear Mrs Milverton,

Oh, dear! I am no financial expert, not by any means, so I asked Dr Watson, but he didn't know what to say, either, so we both consulted Mr Holmes, showing him your letter. What a reaction it produced! Both of my tenants exclaimed, "Milverton! Could it be the same?"

Queries were then set in motion, and I regret to inform you that it has proven to be true that you were married to the worst scoundrel in London's recent history, Mr Charles A. Milverton, who was, according to Mr Holmes, a fiendish blackmailer who was shot by one of his victims.

As for the money he left you, which speaks of a better side of his nature than either Mr Holmes or Dr Watson would have countenanced, there are a few possible things you might do with it. In order of our conjoined advice, they are 1. Turn it in to Scotland Yard and ask them to recompense your late mate's victims, or 2. Invest the money in some worthy cause, or 3. Salt it away or put it in your will.

Sincerely,

Mrs Hudson

⚹　⚹　⚹　⚹

My Dear Mrs Hudson,

I am a native American—more commonly called an Indian, though I am not in any way connected to those Oriental folk. I live in a small town in what you call Mary-land, though we write it without the hyphen. I have saved for many years—decades, really!—in hopes of someday visiting London. Why? Because my curiosity was wakened and nurtured by Washington Irving, Charles Dickens, and other writers.

Now that I am in my late sixties, I find that I can finally indulge my heart-felt wish. In a few months, I shall travel to your splendid city and stay for a full month. It would be a thrill to meet you and your illustrious tenants, but most of my stay shall take me to whatever places you may especially recommend.

Thankfully,

Abigail O'Connor

✗ ✗ ✗

Dear Miss (Mrs?) O'Connor,

I am flattered that you regard my opinion so highly. Unfortunately, neither Mr Holmes or I live in London, but you will find Dr Watson at our old address, so do drop by to meet him, he will be altogether pleased.

As for what you would like to see, the possibilities are endless. I don't suppose you need to be told to take in the Tower of London or the British Museum, but since you express a liking for the late Mr Dickens, you should certainly visit his old home on Doughty Street, which is not far from the museum. I also recommend a day trip to Rochester, where Dickens both was born and died. It is a short train journey of less than an hour. If you should go and manage it in the summer-time, there is a time when all the villagers dress up as Dickensian characters. The main street is about a mile long and has historical markers where various encounters from the novels took place. If you have read his last unfinished novel, *The Mystery of Edwin Drood*, which Mr Holmes says he has personally solved, you will encounter the cathedral, the home where the choir-master Jasper lived, and the very school where Rosa Budd was in attendance, though this is now a museum wholly devoted to Dickens.

Do enjoy your visit!
Mrs Hudson

✗   ✗   ✗   ✗

Dear Mrs Hudson,

I am both a game collector and inventor, and while I am principally involved in board games, I am quite fond of card games. I wonder whether Mr Holmes and Dr Watson play, and if they do, what games do they like best?

Sincerely,
Sidney Abbott

✗   ✗   ✗

Dear Mr Abbott,

I myself enjoy an occasional evening of Whist with my friends, but I have not noticed either of my tenants inviting anyone over to play it. Mr Holmes rarely has time to indulge in such leisurely activities, though I have heard that he is a formidable Chess player, whereas Dr Watson excels at Checkers. Mr Holmes has spoken well of the Japanese game called Go, but I don't know if he has ever played it. Card games in general do not appear to interest Mr Holmes, but Dr Watson enjoys many varieties of Solitaire.

Sportingly,
Mrs Hudson

✗   ✗   ✗   ✗

Dear Mrs Hudson,

I do not know whether you have any experience with any teenage girl, but I hope you have advice as to know to manage a rebellious eighteen-year-old.

Frantic in Fanwood

✗   ✗   ✗

My Dear Frantic Friend,

From time to time, I am visited by one of my nieces, as well as a nephew. Philip is sometimes a bit wild, but Jennifer is a lamb. At any rate, I do urge you to cultivate patience where your daughter (I presume) is concerned. She is on the threshold of becoming a young lady with the upcoming responsibility of self-governance. This means that she will begin to regard you as her model and guide, and this ought to mellow her. And do remember what that Yankee humorist once wrote: "When I was a boy of fourteen, my father was so ignorant I could hardly stand to have the old man around. But when I got to be twenty-one, I was astonished at how much the old man had learned in seven years."

Sympathetically,
Martha Hudson

✗ ✗ ✗ ✗

Dear Mrs Hudson,

Has Inspector Lestrade of Scotland Yard ever joined Mr Holmes and Dr Watson for dinner at 221 Baker Street! If he did, what did you serve him?

Emeric Bassington

✗ ✗ ✗

Dear Mr Bassington,

Yes, there was one occasion when Inspector Lestrade consulted with Mr Holmes and the hour began to grow late, so he was invited to dinner. I asked Mr Holmes for advice on what to prepare, and he said that he was certain that our guest is a man of simple tastes. "But if you can ring in one thing that is a bit unusual, his reaction might be of interest."

Well, I couldn't think of anything more exotic than the cherries in brandy whose recipe appeared in my previous column, so we finished with it for dessert. The rest of the meal was indeed ordinary, though delicious. I intended to serve a simple salad, but Mr Holmes advised me not to, for the inspector's portion would go to waste. Here is the meal I ended up serving. The inspector did enjoy it.

PEA SOUP

1 pound of rinsed dry peas, whole or split, as desired
1 ham bone
1 cup of diced onion
1 cup of diced celery
1 ½ cups of sliced carrots
¼ teaspoon of pepper
8 cups of water

1. Boil the peas uncovered in water for two minutes.

2. Cover the pot for one hour.

3. Add the onion, celery and pepper and stir.

4. Add the ham bone.

5. Boil the soup and then lower the flame.

6. Cook covered for one-and-a-half hours.

7. Take out the ham bone and cut the meat from it, trimming away the fat.

8. Chop the ham into small pieces.

9. Place the ham and carrots into the soup and boil the mixture.

10. Lower the flame and cook for half-an-hour.

✗   ✗   ✗   ✗

ROASTED POTATOES

2 pounds of potatoes
Oil, your preference

1. Fire up the oven to 375 degrees.

2. Peel the potatoes and cut them in half.

3. Boil them in a large pan of salted water.

4. Lower the flame and cook for five minutes.

5. Drain the potatoes and inscribe the skin of each piece with a fork.

6. Put the potatoes into the pan and cover it.

7. Pour enough oil into a big pan till it holds a half-inch of oil.

8. When smoke appears above the oil, put in the potatoes, spreading them into one layer.

9. Coat the potatoes with the oil and bake them for forty minutes. Turn them often.

10. Drain the potatoes and cover them in salt (not too much), then serve them.

✗   ✗   ✗   ✗

STEWED BEEF

2 pounds of cubed beef
1 ½ cups of diced onion
14 ½ ounces of chopped tomatoes, with their juices
6 chopped carrots
1 cup of celery
3 mid-sized peeled and chopped potatoes
3 tablespoons of tapioca
1 diced clove of garlic
1 tablespoon of parsley
1 bay leaf
10 ½ ounces of condensed beef broth
2 tablespoons of oil, your choice
1 teaspoon of salt
¼ teaspoon of pepper

1. Place a batch of beef in oil into a heated Dutch oven.

2. When the beef browns, remove and drain.

3. Repeat steps 1 and 2 till all of the beef is cooked.

4. Place the beef in a pan.

5. Add the bay leaf, broth, garlic, onion, parsley, pepper, salt, tapioca and tomatoes.

6. Boil the mixture.

7. Cover the beef stew and bake it for 1½ hours at 350 degrees.

8. Add the carrots, celery and potatoes and stir the mixture.

9. Remove the bay leaf and serve the stew.

SCREEN OF THE CRIME

by Kim Newman

So, three more episodes of the BBC's *Sherlock* to chew over ... Considering the name of this magazine, I'm assuming you'll have seen the things so won't have any issues with spoilers.

Sherlock has an unusual format in UK and US TV terms—with 'seasons' consisting of just three feature-length episodes doled out every few years. With the increasing profile of stars Benedict Cumberbatch and Martin Freeman in Hobbit and Marvel Comics movies and other Oscar or Emmy-bid material like high-end biopics or seasons of *Fargo*, it is plainly becoming a nightmare of scheduling (and, though no one likes to mention it, cost) to get them both in the same drawing room for long enough to shoot what boils down to three whole films. Creator-producer-writers Steven Moffatt and Mark Gatiss (whose Mycroft here gets bumped up to co-star status with the killing-off of another regular) are also busy these days, so this might be the end of the saga—the series closes not with a cliffhanger (or waterfall-plunger) but a settling into format as the two flawed, traumatised neurotics finally become the case-solving legendary team they are expected to be. It is notoriously difficult to keep up the quality over long run, and Sherlock episodes eat through material—each one tackles a bucketful of cases and elements—at a dizzying rate. If this trio aren't as immediately impressive as earlier seasons (each of which tended to have one dud) and have slipped into mannerisms and a fan-fiction-like obsession with the formative experiences of the regular characters rather than their actual adventures, it's worth remembering that—considering the show as a series of feature films—we've reached a point on a level with *Octopussy, Freddy vs Jason, Carry On Screaming, Godzilla's Revenge, Tarzan and the Huntress* or (most aptly) *The Woman in Green*.

"THE SIX THATCHERS"

The 'previously' montage at the beginning of Series Four of *Sherlock* skips entirely the detour of last year's footnote special ("The Abominable Bride") to pick up threads from "His Last Vow"—a cliffhanger shuffled out of the way sharpish so we can get on with new matters. There's a case involving a corpse who was supposed to be in Tibet (where Doyle's Sherlock wandered for a while) found in a burned-out car in his parents' driveway, which is solved with dazzling ease by Cumberbatch's Sherlock (though why no one checked the lad's travel movements is the sort of mystery the unkind might label a thumping great plot hole) and dropped to pay brief attention to a rethink of "The Six Napoleons." Now it's busts of Margaret Thatcher being smashed and Doyle's mcguffin is sneered at with one of writer Mark Gatiss's many genuinely funny lines ("it's only a pearl—get a new one!"). Inside the sixth bust is an AGRA-labelled flashdrive we saw briefly two years ago (and, okay, to be fair, in the new credits sequence) which reveals that this is all about Mrs. Watson (Amanda Abbington), improbable ex-superspy.

Doyle found marrying Watson off in the second story an annoying hindrance to the series and so very quietly killed her off while Holmes was supposedly dead and then forgot he'd done that so scholars intuit a second (or any other number) Mrs. Watson came along. Here, that translates into Watson (Martin Freeman, a tad underemployed) suffering loss of sleep with a new baby in the house and getting texty flirty with a redhead (Sian Brooke) who smiles at him on a bus and then deciding not to have an affair ... only for the finale to have Mary take a bullet for Sherlock in an aquarium, which prompts Watson to break it off permanently (yes, we believe it!) with Holmes, raising the dread prospect of two more feature-length episodes mostly about getting them inevitably back together again. The fact that Doyle did this stuff with a line or two *and then got on with the mysteries* shows how off-track *Sherlock* has got, to the point that the American *Sherlock* knock-off *Elementary*—which itself got strangled for a season on Sherlock's unnecessary father issues—is currently edging ahead as a crime-solving drama.

It's all still dazzling (as directed by Rachel Talalay, exiled to TV after *Tank Girl* but doing great work), with the regular cast committed to bringing their A games because otherwise they risk being acted into a corner by the others (only Freeman is fading—and that may be because Watson is becoming something of a wet blanket this year), bits of visual and verbal invention which remain priceless and some great tossed-off insights—but this is supposed to be a 'real' story after last year's pretend one (the Victorian fantasy), and as such it's disturbingly insubstantial. There's a lot of guff about taking things personally and "it's not a game any more" with dark hints about a third Holmes sibling (keyword: Sherrinford) and mutterings about the still-dead Moriarty's posthumous plot ... but by ramping up the hero's involvement in stories Holmes used to be detached (or seemingly detached) from, this has somehow turned into soap rather than mystery. It's a prevailing tone—Moffat's *Doctor Who* has gone that road too, and it's by no means uncommon in larger pop culture—but at this point it would be a relief for Holmes to have a client with a puzzling mystery that he comes at from the outside and solves through use of his formidable deductive skills.

Charles Edwards, who played Doyle in *Murder Rooms*, has a nice bit as the grieving Tory minister with a Thatcher shrine and Sacha Dhawan, one of the busiest actors around, is miscast as a hardbitten, maniacal ex-mercenary.

"THE LYING DETECTIVE"

Embedded in this feature-length Moffat-scripted episode is a terrific, pertinent updated version of "The Dying Detective" (the one in which Holmes pretends to be delirious on his death-bed to gull a gloating poisoner) with Sherlock in full-on drug addict mode and again making a fool of himself in public by accusing a villain who seems to be untouchable. Culverton Smith (Toby Jones, with manky false teeth) is super-creepy as a rich serial killer who melds H.H. Holmes (of 'murder hotel' fame), Alan Sugar and Jimmy Savile—a businessman/TV star/philanthropist who has donated a purpose-built hospital to the NHS (it looks a lot like the new wing of Broadcasting House) to afford him access to victims whose deaths will be put down to natural causes. His 'favorite room' is the morgue, where he grotesquely fondles the dead, and he holds tyrannical sway over everyone even remotely in his employ—a repeated bit of business about "how long have you worked here?" is nails-down-a-blackboard unpleasant.

However, this being *Sherlock*, there's no such thing as a stand-alone story and the whole thing is wrapped up in Sherlock trying to shock Watson out of his grief (and their estrangement) by putting himself in such danger that his friend has to respond. John has long chats with his imaginary dead wife—and it seems for a while that Sherlock too has hallucinated an encounter with Smith's daughter, but that's a feint (as is Watson's new shrink) to bring back the girl on the bus from last week who turns out to be … a hitherto-unexpected and demento Holmes sister, who is yet another of Moffat's quixotic-sexy-monster-women (a ton of them have showed up in *Doctor Who* on his watch) and set to drag the show back into the snake-swallowing-itself incestuous tangle next week. This is becoming so focused on the mental states of its leads that even regulars like Molly (Louise Brealey) and Lestrade (Rupert Graves) are being reduced to walk-ons, Mycroft is stuck with a silly fanfic bit as the power player (Lindsay Duncan) he arrested last week comes on to him and the mania for having a hero's firm friends lay into him as a ghastly human being even extends to poor Mrs. Hudson (Una Stubbs), who is here shown to own a flashy Aston Martin (admitting that as the widow of a drug dealer who owns property in central London she's probably well-off) and drives it terribly to get a cheap laugh (it'd be funnier if she had a Bond ride and drove it like a fussy little old lady).

While you're watching, it's effortlessly engaging—and some of the most daring strokes pay off: we literally see two different actresses playing one role and it's not till the first one comes back in a flashback we notice the substitution (well, I didn't) and Jones chews so much scenery as the mocking monster that he'd be un-believable if there weren't horrible real-life precedents to suggest he may be underdoing it. However, in the afterglow, the "but … but … but" and "oh really—he's completely forgotten his own sister" niggles come to the fore. More damaging than this aftereffect, which many of Doyle's own stories have, is that it's all so inner-directed that it's in danger of becoming hermetically sealed.

Doyle's Holmes takes cases and fights for causes ... the world doesn't revolve around him; here, the mere fact of his existence is the motor for 98% of what happens in the show. In the DVD extras, Abbington talks about her character dying and being sorry she won't be working with the show's team again—but, like Andrew Scott's Moriarty—Mary gets to be almost busier post-mortem than she was when alive, deluging 'the boys' (and the viewer) with messages recorded pre-death that nudge the plot along.

"THE FINAL ADVENTURE"

The whole point of the Season Four closer is to push a reset button, to get the series back to its strengths (albeit with a baby Moffat and Gatiss have clearly no interest in plumped into the final montage) by clearing the air between Holmes and Watson and getting through all the family tsuris that has come to dominate the program ... but that means the Sherlock we want to see is confined to a few fan-service glimpses (dancing men!) in a montage and some striding out of Rathbone Place (which looks not at all like the location used here and is incidentally the road off which Newman Passage leads at the beginning of *Peeping Tom*) for a finish. The downside is that the rest of the show is *all* family nonsense about how the literally forgotten Holmes sister Eurus (Greek for 'the East wind', apparently) has been plotting supervillain-style from inside a supposed super-prison island and pulling all manner of strings to wreck her siblings' lives. Her cute parents, played by Ben the C's real Mum (Wanda Ventham of *UFO* and *The Blood Beast Terror*) and Dad (Timothy Carlton), are off-limits for no narrative reason beyond the fact that the writers/creators don't want to stretch stunt casting too far and are reluctant to kill off pet characters entirely, bringing back Mary for a second post-mortem video and Moriarty for the umpteenth scattering of .gif-like tipped-in sneers.

There's a *Silence of the Lambs* reference, an *Arkham Asylum* vibe and sets which pay homage to a Ken Adam design from *Dr. No*, but I suspect the real inspiration for this set-up is the Jon Pertwee *Doctor Who* serial "The Sea Devils," where the Master (the Doctor's version of Moriarty) was sole prisoner on an offshore castle and also managed to get sway over the Governor to continue meddling in the Doctor's life. In his *Doctor Who*, Moffat has turned the Master into Missy … so it should be no surprise that the big bad of this series turns out to be Sissy—who has less character as herself than she did when posing as other people in the set-up episodes (which get forgotten a bit—doesn't Watson remember he used to fancy her?). Last week, while in delirium, Sherlock all but admitted that his deductive ability was a psychic power, and here Miss East Wind Holmes has the sort of mutant ability to influence and control everyone she talks to, which feels more like a Marvel Comics villain (in fact, very like David Tennant's Killgrave from *Jessica Jones*) than someone who can be accommodated within the rational world of Holmes & co. Indeed, the calm deductive reasoning of Doyle has been melded with the ESP-like psychic connection of Thomas Harris's Will Graham—the fact that a way of seeing the world is inherited by all three Holmes siblings makes it much more like a super-power than a rational technique.

With both the creators collaborating on a wrap-up script, there's a lot to get through and many disparate strands to lay in: a girl-on-a-plane false scent that evokes 70s TV like *Doom Watch* or *Department S*; an Evil Clown/Scary Moppet horror movie staged to terrify the unflappable Mycroft; a burned-down family home out of *Skyfall* (with the too-gabbled-to-process version of the Musgrave Ritual the script doesn't have the Doylean patience to work out properly); Japanese gameshow horror tropes with killer puzzles to put Sherlock under mental and moral pressure; an exploding drone in Baker Street (if it had killed the targets, would Sis be disappointed not to be able to use all her other traps and tricks?); micro-bits for the marginalized regulars (could Molly really get past the unforgivable phone trick to be smiley in the final montage?); camp gags about Mycroft (let's face it, Gatiss) playing Lady Bracknell; and a campier flashback turn for Scott's strutting Jim Moriarty as he has a super-villain team-up with Eurus.

And yet, it still boils down to three or four people talking to each other in a concrete room, with enough misdirection and pizzazz to put off the moment when you ask why the Hell a supervillain would bother to devote her whole life to tormenting her own family. And, if she did, since her party piece as a little girl was murdering Sherlock's best friend because she was jealous at not being allowed to join in their pirate games, why isn't her main target *Watson*? The cliffhanger of "The Lying Detective" has her shooting him in the face—but it turns out she didn't mean it and just used a tranquilizer dart. Is it significant that Holmes's childhood best friend's nickname (Redbeard) is the title of an Akira Kurosawa film about the education of a young doctor and a wiser mentor—if so why did he stick himself with the name Yellowbeard, referring to a terrible Graham Chapman comedy? Where were the other super-dangerous prisoners on Sherrinford—shouldn't Eurus have replaced all the guards with psycho-terrorists and superbads, perhaps even including Culverton Smith from last week? Given that the whole show is about people with serious maladjustments and gaps in their emotional range, is it intentional that there's such a dramatic limit to who it can care about—Eurus murders a bunch of human plot tokens (nice bit where she muses that killing the guilty and killing the innocent feel no different) but just because she's a Holmes (a new one we've only just met and have no history with or attachment to) there's supposed to be a tragic dimension to her insanity and we get a violin duet at the end.

I'd assume that if the show ever does come back between *Dr. Strange* sequels, Martin Freeman's US credits and (if there's any justice) Louise Brealey's ascent to international character actress superstardom, the backstory is out of its system and we can get back to cases … except for that ominous note about 'Uncle Rudy', which might bring in still more relatives to keep the squabble going.

✗

Kim Newman is a prolific, award-winning English writer and editor, who also acts, is a film critic, and a London broadcaster. Of his many novels and stories, one of the most famous is *Anno Dracula*.

SHERLOCK HOLMES—IN THE CARDS

by Gary Lovisi

Over the last few years it has been my pleasure to share various Sherlock Holmes items with the readers of this fine magazine. As a collector and author, it is a pleasure to pass on information about unique and fascinating items of Sherlockania. Of course we all know the world of Holmes and Watson is not just limited to stories or books—nor films, magazines or even comic books—but to a plethora of more esoteric items. Some of them are quite interesting and often rare collectables.

A good example is the British Turf Cigarette set of twenty-five cards that were published by Alexander Boguslavsky, Ltd., 55 Piccadilly, London, in 1923. This set of charming antique picture cards is officially named the "Conan Doyle Characters" set, but it might as well have been called the Sherlock Holmes and characters card set because Holmes or characters from The Canon are featured on nineteen of the twenty-five cards. The six exceptions being for characters who appear in Doyle's historical novels. The rest of the cards feature nice color drawings of Sherlock Holmes (with pipe and another card of him in disguise), also Watson, Moriarty, Lestrade, Irene Adler, Tonga, Miss Mary Morstan and many famous characters found in the Holmes stories. The only non-human character card is the hound from *The Hound of The Baskervilles*. The artist is unknown and the art is nice and colorful and gives us tight head shots of each character in the style of cigarette card art of the era.

The Turf Cigarette Cards measure 1 3/8 x 2 5/8 inches in size—the standard size for antique cigarette cards with one card being included in each pack of Turf Cigarettes. Each card is numbered and, of course, card #1 is Sherlock Holmes and card #2 is Holmes in disguise. I assume the card series was authorized by Doyle, who was alive at the time. I also assume that he did not want it to be a Holmes cards series—so it was officially named the Conan Doyle Characters card series and Turf added six other non-Holmes characters. Doyle was particularly proud of his historical novels and so the addition of a Sir Nigel Loring card and a Brigadier Gerard card, among four others, may have met with his approval of the series. Turf didn't always get prior approval for their cigarette cards (i.e. Honus Wagner), however, if permissions were needed, I am sure Doyle would have balked at a card series featuring Holmes and Canonical characters exclusively.

The back of each card has a two or three paragraph description of that character, while the single-story character cards also list the story that character appears in. There seem to be two sets of these cards, one with a green print back and one with a black print back, but I do not know if the color of ink makes one card a first printing or not—it seems not to matter. What does matter is the front cover art showing each character and what is written on the backs of these cards about that character.

The back of card #1 picturing Sherlock Holmes describes the Great Detective thusly:

> *The nature of a detective's work makes it essential that he should avoid publicity. Perhaps that is why no "real life" detective has won the notoriety of Sherlock Holmes, the hero of so many of Sir Arthur Conan Doyle's tales.*
>
> *One cannot help wondering, however, if there exists, outside the pages of history, anyone quite so clever at unraveling mysteries as this remarkable man, with his ingenious methods of work and extraordinary powers of observation.*

The above paragraph must have been written before it was generally known that Dr. Joseph Bell was the template Doyle used for Holmes.

The back of card #2 titled "Sherlock Holmes in Disguise" lists him this way:

> Besides hoodwinking criminals whom he wished to track, Sherlock Holmes used to get fun out of the way in which his disguises deceived even his intimate friends.
>
> In "The Sign of the Four," he appeared as "an aged man, clad in seafaring garb, with an old peajacket buttoned up to his throat," and until he resumed his natural voice Dr. Watson had no suspicion that he was anything but "a respectable master mariner who had fallen into years and poverty."

CONAN DOYLE CHARACTERS

DR. WATSON

Card #3 features Dr. Watson and it describes him in this manner:

Dr. Watson, Sherlock Holmes's friend, often appears unobservant and even a little stupid, in contrast with the famous detective. Those who are inclined to despise him, however, should try their own hand at playing the part of Sherlock Holmes and learn humility!

Holmes was lucky in having a friend who was willing to play second fiddle, yet always ready with his help when required, even if he knew it meant risking his life.

I do not agree with all of the above. Watson was a medical doctor and not "stupid" and I certainly cannot believe there are any Holmes fans who actually "despise" Watson—quite the opposite, but that is the description given on the back of his card.

CONAN DOYLE CHARACTERS

PROFESSOR MORIARTY

Other character cards offer further interesting descriptions. Card #7, Professor Moriarty, tells us:

Professor Moriarty was Sherlock Holmes's arch-enemy, whom the latter once described as "the Napoleon of crime" and recognized as his intellectual equal.

A life-and-death struggle between the two men took place on the edge of a precipice and in order to mislead the members of Dr. Moriarty's gang who were seeking his life, Sherlock Holmes let people go on for several years thinking that he as well as his enemy had been killed.

In the above, "Dr." Moriarty is not a typo of mine—perhaps the card writer confused the Professor with Watson's medical title?

Another important character in The Canon is Irene Adler and her card (#22) describes her thusly:

> *To Sherlock Holmes, Irene Adler was always "the woman"—not because he had fallen in love with her—that emotion being "abhorrent to his cold, precise, but admirably balanced mind"—but because she had seen through his plan of campaign and frustrated it.*
>
> *After meeting this woman, whose brains were a match for his own, we are told that Sherlock Holmes ceased to make merry over the cleverness of women.*

These short back-of-the-card descriptions add to the charm of these cards and I believe they must have been useful to readers who may not have been familiar with all of the Holmes stories or Doyle's other books. They add an important perspective to the character images and the cards themselves.

One note to collectors, all twenty-five cards are shown in black and white on page nine of *The Sherlock Holmes Scrapbook* edited by Peter Haining. Many are also shown in color throughout the pages of *The Sherlock Holmes Companion* by Daniel Smith and the entire nineteen canonical set is shown in color on page seventy in *Sherlock Holmes: A Centenary Celebration* by Allen Eyles.

Below is a complete list of the 1923 British Turf Cigarette Card Set:

#1: Sherlock Holmes

#2: Sherlock Holmes in Disguise

#3: Dr. Watson

#4: Lestrade

#5: Miss Mary Morstan from "The Sign of the Four"

#6: Tonga from "The Sign of the Four"

#7: Professor Moriarty from *Memoirs of Sherlock Holmes*

#8: Lucy Ferrier from "A Study in Scarlet"

#9: Jefferson Hope from "A Study in Scarlet"

#10: Dame Ermyntrude Loring from *Sir Nigel*

#11: Sir Nigel Loring from *Sir Nigel* and *The White Company*

#12: Miss Helen Stoner, from "The Speckled Band"

#13: Dr. Grimsby Roylette from "The Speckled Band"

#14: Mother Superior from *Adventures of Gerard*

#15: Brigadier Gerard from *Adventures of Gerard*

#16: The hound of the Baskervilles from *The Hound of the Baskervilles*

#17: Miss Stapleton from *The Hound of the Baskervilles*

#18: "The Man with the Twisted Lip" from *The Adventures of Sherlock Holmes*

#19: Holly Hinton from *Rodney Stone*

#20: The King of Bohemia from "A Scandal in Bohemia"

#21: Mr. Jabez Wilson from "The Red-Headed League"

#22: Irene Adler from "A Scandal in Bohemia"

#23: Miss Violet Hunter, from "The Copper Beeches"

#24: Rebecca Tayforth from *The Firm of Girdlestone*

#25: Miss Hatty Doran from "The Noble Bachelor"

These lovely little British Turf Cigarette cards can be great fun to collect, but finding them all can be a real challenge to even the most die-hard Sherlockian. First published in 1923, these pretty little cigarette cards are now an amazing 90+ years old, so they have become quite rare. While some cards may be more common than others, all are difficult to find, but they are certainly worth the search for any fan and collector—and who knows—using methods developed by the Great Detective—you may even find sure you will enjoy them.

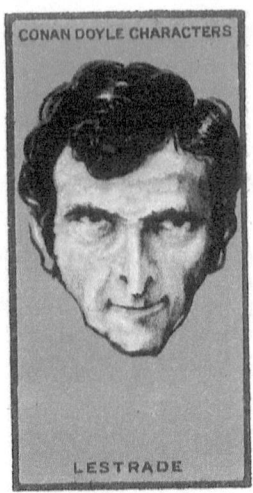

CONAN DOYLE CHARACTERS

LESTRADE

CONAN DOYLE CHARACTERS

TONGA

Gary Lovisi is an MWA Edgar-nominated author for the Best Short Story of the year, for his Sherlock Holmes pastiche "The Adventure of The Missing Detective." He is a Holmes fan, collector, and writes various articles and short stories of, and about, The Great Detective, some of which have appeared in this magazine. He is the editor of *Paperback Parade* and *Hardboiled* magazines, and of the Sherlock Holmes anthology, *The Great Detective: His Further Adventures* (Wildside Press). You can find out more about him and his work at his website: www.gryphonbooks. com, or on Facebook.

THE BABIES IN THE BLIZZARD

A NERO WOLFE DILEMMA

by Archie Goodwin

transcribed by Marvin Kaye

I finished breakfast, got through the mail, caught up with the germination records, which didn't take long because there were so few. Last night Wolfe solved the USB industrial espionage case, so the next thing on my agenda was to deposit the large check for that job.

I wasn't looking forward to trudging over to the bank. It was December and Manhattan was in the middle of a blizzard. There was already fourteen inches of snow, plus frequent hailstorms that broke quite a few car and house windows. I went into the hall and wrapped my favorite scarf around my neck and was about to don my topcoat when the phone rang. I returned to the office and picked it up.

A high thin man's voice said, "Look outside! *Hurry!*"

"Who is this?"

He hung up.

I finished putting on my coat, got my hat and fetched my gloves, but stuck them in my pocket so I could more easily open the front door. I thought about getting my gun, just in case, but the guy didn't sound threatening, so I decided to risk it.

I opened the door and saw snow, snow and more snow. I put on my gloves and was about to step outside when I noticed a wicker basket on the doorsill. I bent down, picked it up, shut the door and examined it. Inside was a milk-filled bottle with a nipple, diapers and a thick wool blanket covering a sleeping infant. I brought my burden into the kitchen.

"Archie," Fritz exclaimed, "what's *that*?"

"Shh ... it's asleep."

"It? *It?*"

"I don't know whether it's a boy or a girl." I set the basket down on the kitchen table. "There are diapers and a bottle of milk." I started out.

"Where are you going?"

"Well," I replied, "I *was* going to the bank, but that'll have to wait. I've got to call and find out if anyone has reported a missing baby. Come to think of it, I'll need to tell them its gender."

Fritz very gently investigated. The child slept on. "It's a girl."

"Thanks." I went to the office and wondered where I should call. If I phoned Cramer, he might laugh enough to bust a gut. I didn't think the problem warranted dialing 911, so reluctantly I rang up the Homicide Bureau.

"Who's been murdered?" Cramer growled.

"No one, or at least not so far as we're concerned. I've got a delicate situation here and don't know who to call. But when I tell you, please don't laugh too hard. Somebody left a baby on our doorstep."

"I'm not laughing. What if it's a kidnapping? That's a federal offense."

"I never thought of that. But then, why would the kidnapper leave her here?"

"Maybe he became panicky."

"Maybe."

"Do you have any details?"

"It's a girl in a wicker basket. There are a few diapers inside and a milk bottle. The child is covered with a grey blanket. She's asleep."

"Good. I'll get—"

"Wait … a man with a high voice called and said, 'Look outside! *Hurry!*' The emphasis was his, not mine."

"Thanks, Archie. I'll phone the proper authorities and they'll get back to you."

He rang off. I was pleased that he hadn't called me Goodwin. So for the present at least, our stock was good.

In a short time, the agency phoned and told me that the baby probably was one just called in by her desperate mother. "We'll be there soon."

And they were. Fritz and I breathed sighs of relief. "Should we tell Wolfe?"

Fritz shook his head. "Maybe later. He's basking in a lucrative job well done."

"You're right." I went to the office and felt I had to tell *someone*, so I called Lily Rowan.

"Oh, Archie, you should have kept her. We'd make wonderful parents!"

I didn't know if she was serious or pulling my leg, so I rang off.

Well, it was a diverting way to begin the work-day, but it was over. I went to the bank, glad to know that charming as that little girl is, we'd seen the last of her.

Or so I thought.

✗   ✗   ✗   ✗

Two days later, late morning. The snowstorm stopped, but a lot of the once-white stuff was now a grimy gray and it was still piled up high.

I was at my desk, contented because I'd finished the mail and for the only time in my memory, there were no germination records. (Have I ever mentioned that doing those records is my least favorite chore?)

And then the phone shattered my mood. It was the same high thin voice.

"Me again. Thanks for trying to help us."

"Us?"

"Me and my wife. Yes, Leanna is my daughter."

"Nice to know her name."

"Now, Archie—"

"You know *my* name?!"

"Obviously."

"So what's yours?"

"Nathan." He didn't volunteer his surname, but I knew I could find out from the agency not only who he is, but where he lives. "Okay, Nat—is that OK?"

"Everybody calls me Nat."

"Thanks. Anything else?"

"Yes. Look outside." And he hung up.

With a groan, I opened the door, expecting to see the same wicker basket. But I was wrong. There were two and of course they contained diapers, milk bottles and a pair of babies. I thought about leaving them there, but it was too cold, so I carried them into the kitchen.

If Fritz's eyes grew any wider, they might have popped out. "*Two?!*"

"One hundred percent for arithmetic. Looks like they're twins."

"This time," Fritz said, "they're awake, but they're both smiling." He picked one up and gave it a bottle.

"That's Leanna."

"How can you tell?"

"Her diaper is pink. This one is blue."

"So that one's a boy."

"Looks like it." We sat quietly for a moment, then I picked up Leanna's brother and supplied him with milk. It was easy—I just did what I saw Fritz do.

"Archie, I think it's time to tell Mr. Wolfe."

I looked for help from heaven, or at least the ceiling. "Guess we'd better. First, though, I'll call the agency."

"Yes—and Archie, you're better at reporting."

"You, sir, are a craven poltroon."

"Such words! Eavesdropping on the master, eh?"

"Oh, go change a diaper!" I put the boy back into the basket and went upstairs to the plant rooms, where Wolfe does not like to be disturbed.

"What now?" he groused.

"You may want to sit down first."

"I'll risk collapsing. Report."

When I told him, he did two things. First, he laughed like I've never seen before. Then he took my advice and sat down. He stifled his mirth and said, "I think, Archie, that I would have preferred a murder."

"Instructions?"

"Call that agency—"

"I already have."

"Good. Then bring me their father."

"What about the mother?"

"Later, perhaps." He rose and began to busy himself with sphagnum, so I beat it.

✗ ✗ ✗ ✗

Nathan Detroit—I swear it!—arrived promptly at nine p.m. As usual, Wolfe waited in the kitchen while I got Daddy seated and brought him the glass of Knob Creek he requested. I complimented him on his choice, then rang the bell for Wolfe.

He entered with Fritz following with a glass and two bottles of Tiger beer. (Wolfe was systematically going —no, *hopping*, pun intended—through Asia, sampling its beers.)

"Mr. Detroit," he said after he sipped and swallowed, "thank you for coming. Please tell us why you are bringing us your twins."

"Actually, Mr. Wolfe, they're triplets. I was going to bring my second girl tomorrow morning."

"Is your wife in on this?"

Nat shook his head. "She has no idea I did it. I hope she never finds out."

"So what's your motive? Perhaps you're only their stepfather?"

"No, they're all mine and I love them."

"What a strange way of showing it!"

"I'm trying to spare my wife," Nat said. "I'm in a lot of trouble."

"Tell us about it." Wolfe glanced at me and I opened my notebook, taking care not to let the father see me taking anything down.

"I had a gambling problem."

"Had?"

"Yes, such a problem doesn't disappear without a lot of help. I joined Gamblers Anonymous. But I still owe fifty thousand to Arthur Mabuse."

"That's bad," said Wolfe.

"Who's this Mabuse?" I asked.

"The descendant of an infamous German gambler, mystic, and racketeer," Wolfe told me. "Combine Professor Moriarty and Arnold Zeck and you've got Mabuse."

"He's a physician?"

"I have no idea what his degree means or even if he has one. But now I understand, Mr. Detroit. Mabuse is quite capable of crippling or murdering your wife and children."

"That's why I brought them to you. I figure this is the safest place possible."

"But what about Mrs. Detroit?"

"She and I were planning to go overseas."

Wolfe shook his head. "That won't help. His organization is everywhere. Probably not in Antarctica, but I wouldn't care to bet on it."

"Then what can we do?"

"Well," Wolfe replied, "you just said it. This *is* the safest place. You may bring your children immediately. But we are not equipped to handle an infant, let alone three."

Nat said, "I'll pay for a nanny."

Wolfe shuddered. "Mr. Detroit, that won't be necessary. The children should be with their parents."

I thought Dad might kiss him. "You mean we—"

"Will stay here. We have a guest room that may be a bit cramped, but I'm sure you'll manage. In the meantime, I will see what we may be able to do about your debt to Dr. Mabuse."

Daddy went home and Wolfe said, "Instructions."

⚡ ⚡ ⚡ ⚡

I wouldn't have found where to go without Purley's help. Of course he wanted to know why. I told him it's for a client.

"Yeah, sure."

"No, really! I swear on my Mom's grave."

"That's a lot of bovine effluent." (No, those weren't his exact words.) "I know that Cramer met your mother."

"Still, I'm not lying."

He smiled for the second time since I've known him. "Just yanking your chain. But look, even though The Angel's dead and one of his sons is a college professor, Giovanni is a mean son of a bitch and he's high in the mob."

⚡ ⚡ ⚡ ⚡

When I first came to New York I became a security guard at a warehouse on a pier along the Hudson. I found out that the guy who hired me was setting me up to be killed by robbers who, instead, caught my bullets. This was during Prohibition and I knew that the warehouse was filled with bootleg liquor supplied by Giuseppe DeAngelo, better known as The Angel. He controlled all the booze in Manhattan. When he found that I'd prevented his warehouse from being emptied, The Angel was so grateful that he kept doing me favors for years. I hoped his son would feel the same way.

Well, he did and he didn't.

I was taken to an elegant living room and sat on a large sofa. DeAngelo entered. He was conservatively dressed. He could easily be mistaken for the president of Harvard or Yale. He smiled and shook my hand, then took a seat opposite me. "Archie, I'm having scotch. What would you like?"

"Scotch on the rocks."

"No, no." He waggled a finger. "This is Matalan 1946 from Macallan. Know what this set me back? Take a guess."

"No idea."

"Four hundred and sixty thousand. I could have bought an island for less." He poured two snifters and handed me one.

"I'm almost afraid to taste it."

"Why?"

"In case my palate isn't up to it."

He laughed. "That'll be our secret."

Due to my ice gaffe, I felt the need to save face, so I said, "Once I was told by a Scottish brewmaster that the best way to experience a single malt is with a few drops of water, preferably from Scotland."

DeAngelo produced a bottle of clear liquid. "This comes from the River Tay in Pitlochry." He poured a little in both glasses, then raised his and clinked it against mine and said, "Slainté!" which he pronounced "slan-jeh." We drank and I could hear the ching-ching of a cash register. As for the scotch, maybe it isn't worth four hundred thousand plus, but it is not a scam. I never saw much reason for having a lot of money, but this was a powerful contrary argument.

"Archie," he said, "normally the only people I see are on business, but you're an exception. Dad always spoke well of you and I've often thought I'd like to meet you. Now how can I be of help?"

I described Nat's problem with Dr. Mabuse and DeAngelo said, "That is one hell of a fix Daddy got himself into. I know all about

Mabuse—he's no doctor or anything else so far as a degree is concerned. As for you and Wolfe, I'm glad to hear how well you're treating the babies. I've got two boys and a girl and I'd do anything to keep them safe and happy."

This was going better than I'd hoped. I asked him if he had any advice on how to deal with Mabuse and he nodded.

"That's easy. Pay him." He stopped me from protesting. "This man is not approachable and if you *could* meet with him, he's totally unreasonable. He has no heart, just a bank account. Since Detroit can't afford to settle his debt, his wife is in danger and next his kids. Fortunately, I can see one way to handle it."

"Yes?"

"I could pay Mabuse."

I was ready to hug him, but the impulse was premature. "You'd do that for him?"

"Detroit? No."

"Then for me?"

"Not even you, Archie. Have some more scotch." He refilled our glasses while I rose. "Where are you going?"

"There's no point staying, is there?"

"Yes." He gave me the glass. "A toast to possibilities."

I humored him. "OK, what possibilities?"

"Really only singular. The possibility that you could make me change my mind."

"I'm listening."

"Dad would have helped you, of course. Fifty thousand was small change to him, as it is for me. But you've used up most of the goodwill from those days. Note that I said most. Because I like you and admire Wolfe I've shared this scotch with you and would do the same for him, though I understand he's a beer and wine man."

"True." I took another sip and decided that if the Greek gods ever discover this stuff, they'll pour their ambrosia into cesspools.

"I've got a problem I can't deal with," DeAngelo said. "If you can solve it, I'll pay Detroit's debt. Even if you can't, I'll consider it a fair deal. But I think you've got the brains, judgment and resources to make a success of it."

"Thanks for your confidence," I replied. "Two questions. Is this something that could lose me my license?"

"No. That sort of thing's my line, not yours. It's strictly legal. Next question?"

"My resources can't possibly match yours. So why—"

He gave me a sad, forlorn smile. "I can't get involved because it involves my brother Tony."

"I've heard he's a teacher at Columbia."

His smile brightened. "Not just a teacher, a professor! Dad was so proud of him and so am I. Though I didn't like it when Tony changed his name, I didn't say anything because when Dad learned he was dying, he made me swear to watch out for Tony, but he also told me, 'No interfering!'"

"Why *did* he change his name?"

"He was afraid that being connected with The Angel would hurt his career. So he became Professor Tad Angelus."

"Wow! I heard him lecture at Columbia. He's brilliant!"

"Archie, stand up." I did and he hugged me. "Never mind about helping Tony, I'm going to call Mabuse and tell him I'll pay his bill."

"But—"

"No buts about it. I can hear Dad telling me to do it. I mean literally."

I shook my head. "You don't mean literally."

"The DeAngelos have powerful vibes," he said and he phoned Mabuse.

Was this the beginning of a beautiful friendship?

When he hung up he said, "Archie, I've got a meeting to attend."

"But you haven't told me about what's troubling your brother."

"You're going to help, anyway?"

"Absolutely."

I asked him if he could be at Wolfe's at nine that evening.

"Sure."

"I have to clear it with him. I'll call and let you know." And with that, I took off.

✗   ✗   ✗   ✗

Wolfe said yes, so at nine we were all in the office—me, Wolfe, Mr. and Mrs. Detroit and even Fritz. The bell rang. I opened the door and saw DeAngelo had two goons with him, but before I could say a word he dismissed them. "Dad told me about Mr. Wolfe's house rules."

When we entered the office, Nat got up and offered the red leather chair to our guest. He accepted it as his due.

"Mr. Wolfe," said he, "thanks for agreeing to see me."

"Well, sir, your father did me a favor that I still appreciate. You see I am having beer. What would you like?"

"Beer is fine. And I know all about that favor. Dad sent you first-rate beer every week during Prohibition."

Wolfe nodded. "That is why both Archie and I will do all we can to help your brother. But tell me this ... must we keep your name out of it?"

"Preferably."

"That might be difficult to do, sir."

DeAngelo sipped while he thought it over. "If you have to tell Tony that I'm involved, go ahead, but only if it's unavoidable."

"Understood. I assume he has an office at Columbia?"

He handed me a 3 x 5 card. "This has got all the data you'll need to contact him." I saw Wolfe wince at what he deems to be an inappropriate use of the word "contact," but for once he let it pass. "Mr. DeAngelo, I'm going to ask Archie to visit your brother, but first we need to know the nature of his trouble."

"I've only heard about it second-hand. I'm sure you need him to tell you directly."

Wolfe nodded. "You're right, of course. But it will help to know the general nature of the problem before we approach Mr. —"

"Professor."

"Professor Angelus."

"All right. I understand Tony's involved with one of his students. She's definitely 'of age.' What he didn't know, though, is that she's married."

"Evidently she didn't wish to share that with him," Wolfe observed.

DeAngelo said yes. "But I had her checked out. She's a good woman and could be right for him. Her husband abused her."

"Physically? Verbally?"

"Every way," he growled. "From what I've heard, she's had black eyes and a lot of bruises. But then he disappeared and after a while she moved out, got her own pad near Columbia and enrolled in their continuing education program."

"I see," said Wolfe. "That is where she met your brother. And after they became involved with each other, her husband reappeared and is blackmailing your brother."

"That's it."

Wolfe refilled his glass and offered more to DeAngelo, but he said he had to get to a meeting.

"Before you leave, sir, I *am* rather curious ..."

"About why I'm not having him taken care of?"

"With your resources, I'd think it likely. But perhaps doing so would run counter to your father's instruction not to interfere with your brother?"

"No, I could handle that. But nobody knows where he is."

"In that case," I said, "it may be more useful for me to talk to her than to your brother."

He handed me a slip of paper. "I figured you'd want to. That's her name, address and contact information."

Again Wolfe repressed a wince.

✗   ✗   ✗   ✗

She picked up on the first ring, which suggested she was waiting for a call.

"Is this Jeanmarie Danette?"

"Who should I tell her is calling?" Careful and canny.

"She's probably never heard of me. My name is Archie Goodwin."

She gasped, not unpleasantly. "Archie Goodwin who works for Nero Wolfe?"

"That's me, Jeanmarie."

She laughed a little. "Never hope to fool a detective. Why are you calling me?"

"I'd appreciate meeting with you at your convenience."

"For what reason?"

"Professor Angelus."

She hung up. I decided to wait a moment before trying again, but I didn't have to. The phone rang and there she was.

"That was rude of me. I'm sorry. You must know about our situation. Could you tell me how you do?"

"Only in person."

"All right," she sighed. "I'm at home."

"I'll be right over." I got the car and headed north to a brownstone apartment two blocks from the Columbia campus. I entered a large living room dominated by, of all things, a loom.

"Yes," she said, "I find it a very relaxing hobby."

"I imagine so." Now that I'd logged in the loom I checked her out. Very thin with very little bust-line, yet her overwhelming quality was a sensuality so intense that I imagined no one involved with her would ever need Viagra.

"Thanks for agreeing to see me. I'm not here in an adversarial capacity. Mr. Wolfe and I want to help you and the Professor."

She poured herself a cup of tea and offered me some. I accepted, took a sip and said, "This is really good!"

"Thanks, Archie. Coming from a man used to Fritz Brenner's cuisine, that's quite a compliment."

"Mr. Wolfe is the gourmet, not me. I don't drink tea all that often. This I could get used to, though. What is it?"

"It's an unfermented tea called gunpowder—appropriate for you, I think. Now tell me this—were you sent here by Tad's brother?"

"So you know about him."

"Yes. Please sit down." She reclined on a chaise longue and I chose an armchair covered in black leather. "Tad didn't tell me about him. Every time I ask about his family, he changes the subject. But I used to be a trade journalist, so I did some digging and learned about The Angel's empire."

"Good, but you probably don't know that when their father died he told Giovanni never to interfere with his brother. That's why he asked me and Wolfe for help. He's hoping his name won't come into it."

"You can bet I won't tell Tad."

"Okay, but I've got to ask you something personal. How do you really feel about him?"

She smiled as if I'd suddenly turned into an archangel. "Not counting my father, Tad is only the second man I've ever loved. I've been married twice. Jimmy, my first husband, was a wonderful man, but he was mugged and died of his injuries. It was a long time before I began dating again."

"To a man who became your second husband?"

"Yes. Chuck Skarrander. I could sense something troubling beneath his surface charm, which he has a lot of. But I finally said yes. I didn't love Chuck, but found him too sexy to resist. We were married and went to Niagara Falls. That night he raped me."

"Didn't that make you want to leave him?"

She sipped tea and shuddered. "Yes, but he frightens me. Night after night he repeated his abuse. In the morning he'd warn me that if I ran away he'd find and kill me."

"Describe him and give me the details of his blackmailing."

She gave me his photo. I asked whether she had any idea where he was staying.

"No idea."

"What about your old Bayonne apartment?"

"He's not there. I sublet it."

I told her to sit tight and do nothing till she heard from me, then I said goodbye.

Outside, I got in my car and waited, but not for long. She headed south, turned right and entered a parking garage. I followed her all the way to Bayonne.

✗   ✗   ✗   ✗

Nine p.m. Wolfe was at his desk and I was at mine. The doorbell rang. I opened it and showed our guest to the front room. Another few minutes and the bell sounded again. Fred brought in an obviously frightened Jeanmarie, followed by Saul with a gun in the back of a furious young man in blue jeans with short brown hair and a long scarred face.

"This is illegal!" he raged as Saul deposited him in a yellow chair.

"Mr. Skarrander," said Wolfe, "this meeting is indeed illegal on your part, but so is blackmail."

"Prove it!" he snapped.

A long sigh. "I will extend the unearned courtesy of asking if you wish some beer, which you see I am having."

"Sure. Why not?"

Wolfe rang and waited for Fritz to accommodate Chuck. Then he said, "Archie, bring in our guest."

I went to the front room and ushered in Giovanni DeAngelo. Chuck was unfazed, but the look Jeanmarie gave me suggested that she had a pretty good idea that the newcomer was Tad's brother.

"Mr. Wolfe," Giovanni said, "will you introduce me to him?"

"Of course. Mr. DeAngelo, this is Chuck Skarrender. Mr. Skarrender, this is Giovanni DeAngelo, head of The Angel's Imports."

Chuck still didn't have a clue, so I told him, "He's the Mafia."

That worried him, but said, "All right, but what does he have to do with me?"

"My brother is Tony DeAngelo."

"Yeah? So?"

"I regret that he changed his name. He's a professor at Columbia ... Tad Angelus."

Chuck jumped up and backed as far away as he could. "I'll give it back! Every penny!"

Giovanni shook his head. "No, you won't. My father said I must never interfere with Tony—Tad. But you won't touch any of it. You won't be anywhere near a bank for quite some time."

"Wolfe!" Chuck shouted. "He'll kill me!"

"No, he won't," he yawned and guzzled beer.

Giovanni went to the front room, opened the door and in came two of his goons. "Mr. Wolfe," he said, "thanks for relaxing your rules this once."

"Just be sure, sir, that they don't harm him."

"Strict orders not to. Take him away, boys." They steered Chuck out the front door. "They'll stay with him all the way to Sicily. He'll be working there in my uncle's mines. And now I'd appreciate some of that beer." Fritz came and went and he sat in his red leather throne. After a few swallows he glared at Jeanmarie. "You were in on it."

She nodded miserably. "I'm still his wife. He said if I didn't hook Tad for him he'd—well, I think you know what he would have done to me."

Wolfe said, "I have an excellent attorney. Divorce is not his line, but I'm sure he'll know someone to get it done quickly."

"Thank you!" she said. "Mr. DeAngelo, I won't blame you for not believing me, but I really do love your brother."

He stopped glaring at her. "My earlier reports about you were all good. I'm going to trust you on this. Forget about Mr. W.'s lawyer. I'll get your divorce by this time next week, maybe sooner." He stood up and shook Wolfe's hand, which he endured. Me he patted on the back. "You handled this beautifully—kept my name out of it. I owe you."

Wolfe demurred. "No, sir, you did my clients the Detroits a great favor."

Giovanni smiled. "But it's almost Christmas."

I followed him to the front door, wondering what we was going to do now that his men were en route to Sicily, but when I opened the door there were two more waiting for him.

✗   ✗   ✗   ✗

Everything worked out well and that's an understatement. Nathan and his wife and kids left the next morning after breakfast. Jeanmarie got her divorce early the next week and Wolfe and I have June invitations to her wedding with Professor Tad.

Our presents from Giovanni DeAngelo came that Sunday and were personally delivered by two of his men. One lugged a case of Remmers beer for Wolfe, the first of a weekly series that's still going on.

The other man carried a large box so gingerly it could have been a bomb. Only it was a bottle of Matalan 1946. It arrived on Christmas Day.

At midnight New Year's Eve even Wolfe had some.

✗

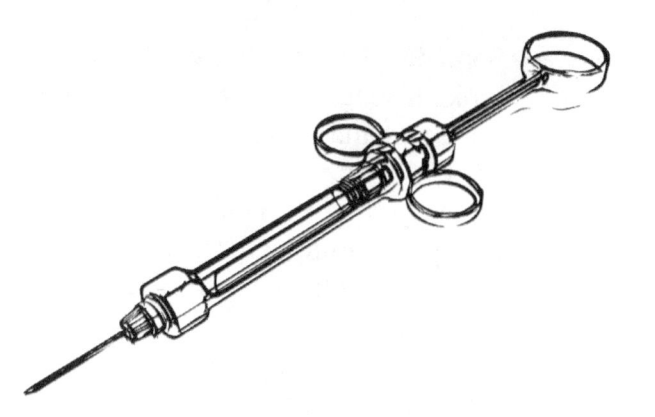

TOO MANY POLITICIANS

A NERO WOLFE RADIO PLAY

by Henry W. Enberg

CAST

(In order of appearance)

ARCHIE GOODWIN, *Wolfe's assistant*
NERO WOLFE, *America's largest detective*
CAROLYN ENDOR, *a murder suspect*
FRITZ BRENNER, *Wolfe's live-in chef*
LON COHEN, *a journalist with* The Gazette
A RECEPTIONIST
MARY KINDEL, *a radio announcer and executive*
ROBERT ROTTERDAM, *a civil rights attorney*
LILY ROWAN, *Archie's special friend*
SENATOR BERNADETTE BUGATTO
STAHL, *an FBI agent*
INSPECTOR CRAMER, *of the New York Police, Homicide Division*
THEODORE HORSTMANN, *Wolfe's orchid nurse*
SAUL PANZER, *Wolfe's favorite independent operative*

✗   ✗   ✗   ✗

ARCHIE: Someday I will tell the story of how Wolfe broke his leg. However, that will be when I am a man of independent means and not while I am still living in his brownstone on West 35th Street, getting paid out of his bank account and eating his grub, as prepared by Fritz Brenner. Not that I am worried about what he would do if I did tell. It's just that I feel a certain responsibility towards him. That's me. Archie Responsible Goodwin. You can take my word for it, though it's a terrific story. Sometimes I'll be walking along the street or sitting at my desk and all of a sudden, I'll start to think about it and … *(Laughs)* Anyway, that afternoon Wolfe was in the office sitting behind his desk with his leg encased in thirty pounds of plaster, propped on a little stool and a heavy oaken cane behind him. He was trying to read *The March of Folly* by Barbara Tuchman. I say trying because at that moment I was at my desk typing replies to orchid fanciers. You see, before he broke his leg … *(Laughs)* … he decided to show me how impervious to my needling he could be by meeting all my attempts to annoy him with an unnatural (for him) calm. It got so that my confidence in my abilities as a gadfly was almost shaken. I was mad. And now I had him at a disadvantage. His leg was broken, he was inconvenienced, he was uncomfortable. So … out came the typewriter. *(Sound of a very noisy typewriter)* This was a sore point with Wolfe at the best of times. I was waiting for a reaction, rather for a particular kind of reaction.

WOLFE: Archie …

ARCHIE: He snapped. That wasn't it.

WOLFE: Archie!

ARCHIE: He growled. *That* wasn't it. I was waiting for the bellow.

WOLFE: ARRRCHIEEEE!!

ARCHIE: That was it. *(The typing stops)* I'm sorry, sir, but I couldn't hear you over the typewriter. *(Aside)* He glared at me. *(In his normal tone)* I've never known it to be this loud. Could it be the kind of typing? I mean, could personal letters be louder than business letters or invoices or …

WOLFE:	Archie.
ARCHIE:	Yes, sir?
WOLFE:	Archie, you know my feelings about pity. It is a useless, repugnant, morally indefensible emotion. Therefore I shall not ask for pity. Rather, I ask only for the consideration due to a man in my present situation.
ARCHIE:	Yes, sir, that's me. Archie Considerate Goodwin. I know a lot of considerate people. In fact, I was talking to Lily Rowan and she considerately offered to come over and sign your cast.
WOLFE:	Good God!

(The sound of a doorbell.)

ARCHIE:	The doorbell rang. I went to the front door and looked through the one-way glass panel. It was a young woman. I recognized the face immediately, so I spent some time looking over the rest. She was dressed for summer in New York, which meant briefly. She had a form that could get away with it very nicely. *(He opens the door)* Yes?
CAROLYN:	You must be Archie Goodwin. I'm Carolyn Endor.
ARCHIE:	I am and I know. I've seen your picture in the papers.
CAROLYN:	I want to see Nero Wolfe.
ARCHIE:	Everyone does. But you're in luck today. We're having a special. All attractive young women are admitted free. Follow me, please. *(Aside)* I didn't tell her that I was taking her in expressly to annoy Wolfe. Never bother a prospective

client with details. *(In his normal voice)* There he is. Nero Wolfe. A captive audience.

WOLFE: Archie! This is the final indignity. How dare you …

CAROLYN: Mr. Wolfe, I'm Carolyn Endor.

WOLFE: *(Oddly)* Carolyn Endor. Indeed. Please, Miss Endor, sit down. You must excuse my outburst, but as you see, I am saddled with an infirmity and with my broken leg, two infirmities.

ARCHIE: He's being witty, Miss Endor. He means me.

WOLFE: However, Archie, I must commend your judgment and thank you for admitting Miss Endor.

ARCHIE: *What?!*

WOLFE: Come, Archie. Pretense does not become you. Of course you know … but perhaps you don't know.

ARCHIE: Know what?

CAROLYN: Mr. Wolfe, you must help me. I know your services are expensive, but I am willing to pay.

WOLFE: Let us leave the question of my fee open, Miss Endor. Archie, your notebook. *(A pause)* Archie? Your notebook.

ARCHIE: He had to repeat himself because I was standing with my mouth open staring at him. Leaving the question of his fee open? Commending my judgment?

Thanking me for letting in a beautiful woman who by *his* standards was practically naked? The fat slob had outdone himself.

WOLFE: Archie!

ARCHIE:	Mr. Wolfe, I am resigning. I am no longer of any use to you. My needle is no good any more. Your skin has grown too tough.
WOLFE:	Not now, Archie, we have work to do. Your notebook, please.
ARCHIE:	What could I do? I sat down, got out a new notebook and faced Carolyn Endor.
WOLFE:	Please state your case, Miss Endor.
CAROLYN:	Surely you must know from the newspapers.
WOLFE:	I wish to hear *your* account. Speak clearly so that Mr. Goodwin can get every word.
ARCHIE:	I had a comeback all ready, but swallowed it.
CAROLYN:	As you probably know, I am administrative assistant to Senator Bernadette Bugatto, who is running for reelection this year. I am also an author. Science fiction, short stories, one novel that sold pretty well. So you see, I am fairly successful.
WOLFE:	Success, Miss Endor, is relative to expectation.
CAROLYN:	I mean that I am established within the mainstream of society.
WOLFE:	Ah.
CAROLYN:	That wasn't always true. In college—Yale—I was involved with radical elements. That's where I met Ashley Mordred, the man who … who they say I murdered.
WOLFE:	They have done more than say so, Miss Endor. You have been indicted, have you not?
CAROLYN:	Yes, Mr. Wolfe.

WOLFE:	And yet you are free to come here and consult me.
CAROLYN:	That is due to Bernie ... Senator Bugatto's influence. She's been wonderful. She could have cut me ... it would have been expedient for her to do so.
WOLFE:	Now the circumstances of the murder.
CAROLYN:	Ashley was murdered in his apartment in the West Village three weeks ago Sunday. He was shot twice. His landlord heard the shots and found him.
WOLFE:	And the evidence against you?
CAROLYN:	He was shot with my gun. It was found beside his body along with certain personal papers of mine, which I thought were in my desk at my office.
WOLFE:	*(Sarcastically)* I trust that the police thanked you for leaving such clear evidence of your guilt.
CAROLYN:	They say I heard the landlord coming and panicked. They say it was a crime of passion.
WOLFE:	Were you and Mr. Mordred intimate?
CAROLYN:	We *were* in college. But when I broke with the radical movement, I broke with Ashley.
WOLFE:	Have you an alibi for the time of the murder?
CAROLYN:	No. I was cleaning my apartment.
WOLFE:	And what is it that you would like me to do?
CAROLYN:	I am innocent, Mr. Wolfe. I want you to find the real murderer

WOLFE: But surely you have a lawyer, Miss Endor. Have you faith in his abilities?

CAROLYN: It's not that. You see, my attorney is Robert Rotterdam.

WOLFE: Indeed. Yale Law School and the Legal Aid Society.

CAROLYN: You know him.

WOLFE: I know of him.

CAROLYN: Then you know how flamboyant he can be. He wants to turn this case into an indictment of the legal system. I don't. It might hurt Senator Bugatto's chances for reelection.

WOLFE: Why don't you dismiss him, then, and get another lawyer?

CAROLYN: Robert's been very good to me. He got me my first job out of law school with Legal Aid and my job with Senator Bugatto. And besides he … he …

WOLFE: You are as incapable of guile as Mr. Goodwin. Mr. Rotterdam, then, replaced Mr. Mordred in your affections.

CAROLYN: Yes. In my last year of law school. Robert … Mr. Rotterdam is the one who convinced me to work within the system.

WOLFE: The system that he is trying to indict. Was there no other reason for your rift with Mr. Mordred?

CAROLYN: I met Ashley in my first year of law school. Soon after, my mother died. My father took an unreasonable dislike to Ashley. I was never close to him—my father. I mean—and he's famous for not showing what's going on inside

his head—but I think he actually hated Ashley—almost enough to kill him.

ARCHIE: Wolfe's eyebrows went up a whole quarter of
             an inch at this! He was stunned.

WOLFE: Then you suspect your father of ...?

CAROLYN: I don't know what to suspect, Mr. Wolfe. Or
             think.

WOLFE: Miss Endor, I *shall* take your case. Is Senator
             Bugatto in the city?

CAROLYN: Yes, she's campaigning here for the next few
             days.

WOLFE: Good. Archie, you will contact Senator Bugatto.
             Also Mr. Rotterdam. I need a thread to pull. Use
             your experience guided by your intelligence.

ARCHIE: After Wolfe's performance, I wasn't ready to
             trust either any more.

WOLFE: Is Mr. Cohen at *The Gazette* under any obliga-
             tion to us?

ARCHIE: If he isn't, I'll twist his arm.

WOLFE: Unnecessary. Find out about Mordred. Any oth-
             er background information would be welcome.

ARCHIE: That's me. Archie Background Good—

WOLFE: And call Saul Panzer. Have him come here at
             eleven o'clock tomorrow morning.

CAROLYN: Mr. Wolfe ...

WOLFE: You can use the telephone in the kitchen.

CAROLYN: Mr. Wolfe, I ...

WOLFE: Please, Miss Endor. Go, Archie!

ARCHIE:	I went. I wanted to think. This was an entirely new Wolfe. Tolerant. Relaxed. Amiable. Insufferable. In the kitchen, Fritz was chopping mushrooms.
FRITZ:	Hallo, Archie.
ARCHIE:	Don't tell me what's for lunch, Fritz, because I won't be here.
FRITZ:	Oh? A client?
ARCHIE:	A client.
FRITZ:	But, Archie! What about his leg?
ARCHIE:	What about it? The only part of his anatomy liable to be injured from working is too well-padded to matter. *(Aside)* I called Saul Panzer, but he was out. I left a message with his answering service. *(The sound of a buzzer)* That was the buzzer calling Fritz to the office. I followed.
FRITZ:	Yes, sir?
WOLFE:	This is Miss Endor, Fritz. She will be staying to lunch. Mr. Goodwin, however, will not. There will be no change therefore in the number of settings, but there will be in the amount of food. The chicken livers, is it not?
FRITZ:	Yes, sir.
WOLFE:	You will save some for Mr. Goodwin.
ARCHIE:	No, thanks. I've lost my appetite. If I get hungry, I'll grab a sandwich somewhere.
WOLFE:	As you wish.
ARCHIE:	*(Sputtering)* As I ... as I ... *(Singing through gritted teeth)* As I wandered out on the streets of Laredo, as I wandered out in Laredo one day ...

ARCHIE: Lon Cohen's office is just down the hall from the publisher of *The Gazette*. It looked the way it always looked, except now there was a computer terminal. *(To Lon)* I'm glad to see you're well equipped. I suppose you play Pac Man in the afternoons. Or did that thing tell you to raise on a pair of queens ace high?

LON: You're just bitter because I took the pot last week.

ARCHIE: I'll let that pass in silence. What do you know about Ashley Mordred beyond the fact that one of his parents liked *Gone With the Wind*?

LON: It's a family name. His grandfather was an Ashley. As to his murder, *The Gazette*'s thirty-five cents on any newsstand. Besides, since when has Wolfe been taking political cases? If you're here because Wolfe's working for Carolyn Endor, there's no way she could pay his fees.

ARCHIE: Actually, Wolfe *is* working for Miss Endor.

LON: Tell me more.

ARCHIE: If you give me the inside dope on the late lamented.

LON: Throw in reports of the investigation and an exclusive interview with Wolfe when he gets the killer and I might.

ARCHIE: We may be able to work something out, although I think you owe me one.

LON: Possibly, especially when you keep folding on two kings.

ARCHIE: I continued my outraged silence. But I will tell you why Wolfe's working for Carolyn

Endor—she has a secret power learned in the Orient to cloud men's minds so they can deny her nothing.

LON: All right, you don't want to tell me. You never do.

ARCHIE: I'm being serious. I took her in to see Wolfe. She introduced herself. And that old phony started acting as if she'd grown an orchid with stars and stripes.

LON: Of course she could be one of those people who can charm their way in anywhere. You know, young man, I like your face. Maybe you're one of those people. In any event, I will unload. I do want that exclusive, though.

ARCHIE: The way this case has been going, Wolfe will come here and deliver it in person.

LON: Ashley Mordred was a poor little rich kid. He went away to Yale for college with Guy Angleton. *(A pregnant pause)*

ARCHIE: Am I supposed to gasp in disbelief? Who is Guy Angleton?

LON: For someone who's supposed to have the best memory in the free world, you're awfully bad on names. In 1978, his senior year at Yale, Guy Angleton joined a terrorist holdover from the Sixties. Liberation blew up things: banks, stuff like that. In April 1979, Liberation assassinated a retired Latin American dictator. One of the hitmen started talking and Guy Angleton disappeared. The FBI's been following up on him ever since—but they never seem to arrive in time.

ARCHIE: Okay, Mordred roomed with Angleton. Miss Endor—actually, if I keep putting on weight,

	I'll probably start calling her Carolyn—had a fling with Mordred. Was it some sort of kinky arrangement?
LON:	Not what I'd call *kinky*. Miss Endor was in the law school and lived off campus. Mordred may have stayed over, but … As I was about to say, the three met at rallies and demonstrations and hit it off pretty well.
ARCHIE:	So we have reds under and on the bed. I suppose they handed out leaflets and manned booths and all the usual stuff?
LON:	As far as I can tell, yes. My sources lost track of them in the fall of 1978, but we do know that Carolyn Endor cleaned up her act. She campaigned in New York for Senator Bugatto that year.
ARCHIE:	A radical like her? I know the senator's supposed to be a liberal, but even her opponent Febrini hasn't called her a Commie. Why would a movement person work for her?
LON:	In two words, Robert Rotterdam. Robert Rotterdam is a noted civil rights lawyer, he—
ARCHIE:	I know he's a lawyer and that he's defending Miss Endor.
LON:	Archie, you surprise me. Rotterdam went to Yale Law with Senator Bugatto some years before. He was there teaching in 1978 and 1979. He talked a lot of Yalies, including Carolyn Endor, into working for the Bugatto campaign. It's the most right-wing thing he ever did. I take that back. Ashley Mordred always said it was Rotterdam who talked him into breaking with the Left. If so, that was pretty right-wing.
ARCHIE:	"If so?"

LON:	My sources have their doubts about the great conversion. Anyway, about this time Mordred moved out on Carolyn—and some say Rotterdam moved in.
ARCHIE:	So Mordred sees the light. Angleton disappears. Carolyn Endor goes to work within the system. And Rotterdam ... gives speeches.
LON:	Right.
ARCHIE:	And for the past five years Mordred—
LON:	—has signed up for every right-wing cause there is. He went to work for a New York tabloid. Nothing much happened until early this year. The paper was digging up the dirt on Senator Bugatto's past for one of those smears it does so well.
ARCHIE:	And Mordred was assigned to it?
LON:	Gotcha! No. He fought it all the way. Then a day or two before he was shot, he changed his mind. Part of the Bugatto file was in his apartment when the police came.
ARCHIE:	So Cramer figures Endor heard about this and wasted Mordred before he could discover some deep dark secret from their Yale days to destroy the senator or her, thoughtfully dropping clues all over the murder scene.
LON:	You've got it. Now I do have some work to do here. Oh, by the way, is Wolfe using Saul Panzer on this one?
ARCHIE:	Of course. First class all the way.
LON:	But Archie— *(The sound of the telephone)* That does it! Out! Out! Out!!!

ARCHIE:	I've got to talk to Rotterdam and the senator. Where are they?
LON:	Rotterdam's probably taping his weekly radio show at WCBJ. Senator Bugatto's going to be at a fundraiser for some fat cats. I don't know if they'd let you in, though.
ARCHIE:	I can get in anywhere. Where's the fundraiser?
LON:	At the penthouse of the senator's biggest supporter, Lily Rowan. Now get out before I call security.
ARCHIE:	Radio station WCBJ is only ten blocks from *The Gazette* and it was shaping up for a pleasant evening, so I hiked through Times Square and up Seventh Avenue. I have always liked the irony about radio stations in New York: the stodgy establishment station's over a betting parlor. They sell overpriced cowhide under the contemporary music outlet and WCBJ, known to its friends as the voice of radical youth and "The Truth That They Couldn't Silence" is over a bank in one of those anonymous office buildings in the mid-fifties one floor above the law firm that invented greenmail. *(The sound of footsteps)* I've always thought that *Monthly Review* was much more entertaining when they had centerfolds of record-breaking tractor drivers.
RECEPTIONIST:	Excuse me?
ARCHIE:	Nothing. I'm Archie Goodwin. I was told that Robert Rotterdam is here.
RECEPTIONIST:	Yes, he's in studio B taping his weekly program. You can wait in the office. He'll be finished in a moment.
ARCHIE:	Is there somewhere I can hear him?

RECEPTIONIST: Well, the Vegetarian Gay Chamber Music Hour is on the air now. I know you can listen in the control room—third door on the left.

(The sound of footsteps and a door opening.)

ROTTERDAM: *(Filtered)* —and can you *blame* them? The booty of their suffering was a skyscraper on Park Avenue; they picked the fruit and from their pain, as I said, came fifty-three years of bloated capitalist profits. In agony they struggled on to ten at night; in hurt, each day was a Monday or a Tuesday, but never was there a respite, never were they *happy*. And nothing was changed in El Salvador—the Fourteen Families and their death squads, the war of an army against the people, the imperialist vultures in Washington circling above murdered nuns. Next week I shall explain why no *blame* attaches to the PLO and how they rose from pain by turning to the bomb.

KINDEL: You have just heard Robert Rotterdam, noted civil rights attorney and crusader for social justice. Professor Rotterdam will be back on this station at the same time next week with another report to the people.

(The sound of footsteps and doors.)

ROTTERDAM: How did it go?

KINDEL: On the nose, as always.

ROTTERDAM: Of course. I must run, dear.

ARCHIE: Hello, Mr. Rotterdam. I'm Archie Goodwin.

ROTTERDAM: How fortunate for you, but should I care?

ARCHIE:	I work for Nero Wolfe and since your client Carolyn Endor—remember her?—hired Wolfe, maybe you should.
ROTTERDAM:	I told her ... indeed, perhaps you are right. Since your employer specializes in crimes of the rich, however, and Carolyn is neither guilty nor rich, I do not think I can help you. I make it my invariable practice not to speak to parasites and *a fortiori* certainly not to assistant parasites.
ARCHIE:	Well, I don't talk to lawyers. Nathaniel Parker's the only one I've ever met who shouldn't be licensed by the FDA as a nonaddictive sleeping potion.
ROTTERDAM:	It must be the big words they use, like "civil rights." It would indubitably be a pleasure to extend our acquaintanceship, Mr. Goodwin, but the Crisis Committee is meeting and I must not be late.
ARCHIE:	Have a nice crisis.

(The sound of footsteps and a door opening and closing.)

KINDEL:	I was hoping you'd do it.
ARCHIE:	What? Deck him?
KINDEL:	At least crack the veneer.
ARCHIE:	*You* called him the noted crusader.
KINDEL:	Oh, he's noted enough and he's been on every crusade since fluoridation ... excuse me, he liked that.
ARCHIE:	As they say in the movies, "You're beautiful in your wrath."
KINDEL:	You say that to all the—
ARCHIE:	Techies?

KINDEL: There's a union rule against that.

ARCHIE: I would hope.

KINDEL: Okay, we've made witty romantic banter. Why are you still here?

ARCHIE: I want to learn radio.

KINDEL: In the beginning, God created Sarnoff and he saw that it was good. And Sarnoff begat Paley and Paley begat Silverman and Silverman begat Tinker and—

ARCHIE: A, that's TV. B, we're not on Sixth Avenue with the networks. C, can you dance?

KINDEL: Huh?

ARCHIE: I cannot learn as much as how to turn on the set unless I have danced with my instructor for a minimum of three hours at the Flamingo Club.

KINDEL: It's tempting, but I'm married. What do you want to know?

ARCHIE: Does Rotterdam always tape his shows like this?

KINDEL: Yes and it's strange. He's always on time to the second and he never messes up a line.

ARCHIE: Never?

KINDEL: Four or five times in three years he's changed his mind and done the show live, but it wasn't to correct anything and those shows timed out, too.

ARCHIE: What do you mean he changed his mind?

KINDEL: Usually—no, always, what he does is answer new letters at the top of the show.

ARCHIE:	Pretend I never heard the program and—
KINDEL:	Have you ever heard it?
ARCHIE:	All right, I confess. Your ruthless cross examination has broken my will. Until this morning I thought a Robert Rotterdam was a Harvey Wallbanger made with Dutch gin.
KINDEL:	(Chuckling) May I use that? Actually, I've pretty much described the show already. "Rotter" reads a letter or two, makes a little speech and then launches into his polemic.
ARCHIE:	What are the letters like?
KINDEL:	Usually from some radical group—the Berkeley 7 or the Atlanta 4 or like that. Sometimes they come from an individual. I remember when he read one from Guy Angleton, you've heard of him?
ARCHIE:	Sure, and this time I mean it.
KINDEL:	Well, Angleton was on the run after that assassination, but he stayed put long enough to ask Rotterdam how the labor theory of value applies to computers. What an idiot!
ARCHIE:	How do you remember that?
KINDEL:	Because the FBI came to the station. They asked to hear the tape. I must have played it for them a half-dozen times.
ARCHIE:	Can't they work a tape recorder? It must be tough when they bug a phone.
KINDEL:	The station wouldn't let them touch the tape without a court order. Anyone else, okay, but not the Feds.

RECEPTIONIST: *(Filtered)* Mary Kindel, Mary Kindel, please report to studio A immediately. The people on the Peace and Love channel have started throwing things. You'd better get in there.

KINDEL: That happens every other week, but I'd better go. See you.

ARCHIE: I'll miss the dancing.

KINDEL: Let's do it. Do you tango?

ARCHIE: Sure. What about your husband?

KINDEL: Through the miracle of modern radio, he has disappeared as if he never existed.

(The sound of a door closing.)

ARCHIE: There was enough time to walk to Lily Rowan's penthouse and the day was still fine, so walk I did. The fundraiser was in full swing when I got there.

(The sound of a door opening. Party sounds.)

LILY: Escamillo! I had no idea that you were politically minded.

ARCHIE: I'm not. I was reading *The Gazette* and saw Senator Bugatto's picture and something snapped. I rushed right over to propose marriage to her. I may even vote for her, if that's what it takes.

LILY: I hope you'll be very happy together. Come in. Of course, you'll have to pay me to keep my mouth shut about your sordid past.

ARCHIE: I couldn't afford it. In fact, Nero Wolfe couldn't afford it. We'd better keep it strictly business, despite my broken heart.

LILY: Business? Nero Wolfe's business?

ARCHIE:	I have no other. Where is Senator Bugatto?
LILY:	I don't know if she'll talk to you here. She's campaigning.
ARCHIE:	Leave that to me. I'll use my charm.
LILY:	In public, Escamillo? I have guests.
ARCHIE:	Just lead me to the candidate.
LILY:	Oh, Senator? Senator Bugatto.
BUGATTO:	Yes, Lily?
LILY:	Senator, I'd like you to meet Archie Goodwin.
BUGATTO:	*(Brisk)* Glad you could be here, Mr. Goodwin.
ARCHIE:	So am I, Senator. We have a mutual acquaintance. Carolyn Endor.
BUGATTO:	*(Wary)* Oh?
ARCHIE:	That's why I wanted to talk to you.
BUGATTO:	I have no comment on the trial.
ARCHIE:	That's all right. Nero Wolfe has enough comments to go around and he wants you to hear some of them.
BUGATTO:	Nero Wolfe?
ARCHIE:	Yes. Carolyn Endor has hired him to discover the real murderer of Ashley Mordred. If there is somewhere that we can go for two minutes, I can explain in more detail.
BUGATTO:	Well …
LILY:	Senator, I know Nero Wolfe. I think you should talk to Mr. Goodwin.
BUGATTO:	*(After a pause)* All right.

LILY: You can use the bedroom. This way. I'll cover for you, Senator.

(The sound of footsteps and then a door opens and closes. The party sounds end.)

BUGATTO: I'm listening, Mr. Goodwin.

ARCHIE: First of all, Senator, for reasons of his own which he won't even tell me, Nero Wolfe thinks that Miss Endor is innocent. You must also, since you haven't deserted her and even used your influence to get her released.

BUGATTO: Of course she's innocent.

ARCHIE: You must have some reason for thinking that.

BUGATTO: I *know* Carolyn. She's been a great help to me and I trust her completely. I don't have any legal evidence, if that's what you're thinking.

ARCHIE: It must be very difficult, especially in the middle of a campaign, to have an aide indicted for murder.

BUGATTO: It's a liability, certainly. My opponent is making the most of it. But once she's acquitted, I can turn it around on him.

ARCHIE: But doesn't the fact that she once rubbed elbows with radicals at Yale—

BUGATTO: Mr. Goodwin, *everyone* in politics has college associations which they would like forgotten. There are more dangerous issues at stake here than that. Dangerous to my campaign, that is.

ARCHIE: Such as?

BUGATTO: Such as the fact that the victim Ashley Mordred also worked in my first campaign six years ago. Such as that Mr. Rotterdam, Carolyn's attorney, wants to play up the political aspects of this case.

ARCHIE: And you don't agree.

BUGATTO: With Rotterdam? I rarely agree with him. The man's a lunatic. He's one of the reasons for the conservative backlash in this country. He gives liberals a bad name. But don't quote me.

ARCHIE: So Ashley Mordred also worked for you. Hmm. Did a man called Guy Angleton?

BUGATTO: Guy Angleton? Yes, he did. How is he involved with this?

ARCHIE: His name keeps popping up. You don't happen to know where I can find him?

BUGATTO: No. He stopped working for me the same time that Ashley did.

ARCHIE: I see. One more question, Senator. Do you think it's possible that your opponent or someone close to him framed Miss Endor to make you look bad?

BUGATTO: No. Bill Febrini hasn't got the imagination or the backbone. As for one of his people ... well, it's an awfully big risk to take.

ARCHIE: I see.

BUGATTO: What I said about Bill Febrini—don't quote me.

ARCHIE: My lips are sealed. Thank you, Senator.

BUGATTO: Mr. Goodwin.

ARCHIE: Yes?

BUGATTO: This has not been an easy campaign for me and I have a long hard fight ahead. I need all of the advantages I can get. But first and foremost I want to see Carolyn Endor cleared. And whatever you and Nero Wolfe have to do, do it. Clear her, Mr. Goodwin.

ARCHIE: We'll do our best, Senator.

✗ ✗ ✗ ✗

ARCHIE: My program completed, I went back to West 35th Street to report to Wolfe. I thought that a full day would cool me down, but was still annoyed. Wolfe's behavior didn't help any. It was a little after 6:30 when I got home and Wolfe was in the office resting. He didn't look up and I didn't volunteer any conversation. *I* wasn't going to give in. Not me. *(Silence)* Not me. *(Silence)* Nope. *(Silence)* Well, I solved the case.

WOLFE: Indeed.

ARCHIE: Yes, but since you're such a genius and you employ me, I'm going to give you a sporting chance. Would you like to hear the evidence or can you read it in my eyes?

WOLFE: You wish to report?

ARCHIE: Well, I can take it or let it alone. But since you sent me out and you are paying me for it—

WOLFE: Proceed, then. Verbatim.

ARCHIE: So I did. It took me thirty minutes. A long time. I got so that I could report long five-way conversations verbatim, complete with inflections and pauses. Now I'm working on facial expressions. After I finished, I said, "Well? Any thread?"

WOLFE: No. Rather, a dynamic within which a thread may be grasped. I expected no more.

ARCHIE: I'm glad to hear that you're happy. And what did you do all afternoon?

WOLFE: I indulged my infirmity. Surely you expected no more. To be precise, I had lunch, conducted Miss Endor through the plant rooms—

(The doorbell rings.)

ARCHIE: I was glad when the doorbell rang. Wolfe was enjoying himself too much. So when I saw who it was through the one-way glass, I suddenly felt very hospitable. *(The door opens)* Well, Mr. Stahl. And how are things at the FBI?

STAHL: Good evening, Mr. Goodwin. May I see Mr. Wolfe?

ARCHIE: Why, sure. We're having open house. Come in.

(The door closes, then footsteps.)

WOLFE: Archie, you are repeating yourself. A tactical error.

ARCHIE: You remember Mr. Stahl, sir.

WOLFE: Of course. Please be seated, Mr. Stahl.

STAHL: I will not stay long.

WOLFE: Be seated, nevertheless. I prefer eyes on a level. Thank you. Now what can I do for you, sir?

STAHL: You are investigating the murder of Ashley Mordred.

WOLFE: Are you asking me to confirm a fact?

STAHL: I'm asking you to cease your investigation.

WOLFE: Indeed. On what grounds?

STAHL: On the grounds of national security.

WOLFE:	Is it in the interest of national security for an innocent woman to be indicted for murder?
STAHL:	Carolyn Endor? She will not come to trial.
WOLFE:	Her attorney will press for a speedy acquittal.
STAHL:	Her attorney has no say in the matter.
WOLFE:	Her employer Senator Bugatto wants a speedy acquittal, also.
STAHL:	I assure you that the interest of justice will be served.
WOLFE:	I prefer to rely on the American judicial system rather the assurances of an executive, especially of a bureau whose sense of honor has often been subordinate to—
STAHL:	Mr. Wolfe. This is a serious matter. Failure to cooperate will cast suspicion in certain circles upon your sympathies.
WOLFE:	Pfui! My sympathies are well-known. My past activities have demonstrated them beyond all suspicion. While I do not imagine myself invulnerable, I might remind you of an earlier confrontation between myself and your agency and of the agreement that resulted. True, circumstances change and any administration that can declare catsup a vegetable is unacquainted with the basic concepts of decency, but—

(Distant gunfire.)

STAHL:	What was that?!
WOLFE:	Archie!
ARCHIE:	Going!!
STAHL:	I'm going with you.

ARCHIE:	I went to my desk and got my Marley, then went to the front door. I looked out the glass and then opened the door. Stahl was behind me. It was the body of a man face down on our steps with two holes in the back of his jacket. He wasn't moving. I carefully lifted his head. I didn't know him. *(To Stahl)* Do you know him?
STAHL:	No.
WOLFE:	*(Off)* Archie!!
ARCHIE:	*(Calling)* Coming!

(The door closes. Footsteps.)

WOLFE:	Well?
ARCHIE:	Dead. I don't know him. Five will get you a hundred that Mr. Stahl does.
WOLFE:	Well, Mr. Stahl?
STAHL:	No.
WOLFE:	I see. Archie, call Mr. Cramer.
STAHL:	Wolfe!
WOLFE:	I am doing my duty as a citizen, Mr. Stahl.
STAHL:	Our meeting must be treated as confidential.
WOLFE:	I must tell the police what I know.
STAHL:	Wolfe!
WOLFE:	If you do not wish to be found here, Mr. Stahl, I suggest you leave now. Someone else must have heard the shots. The police are probably on their way even now.
STAHL:	Have you a back way?
WOLFE:	Fritz will show you. Archie, the phone.

ARCHIE:	Of course dinner was ruined. When the cops showed up, a crew went right to work on the doorstep and our visitor and Cramer went right in to talk to Wolfe. I watched the lab boys for a while and then went into the office where …
CRAMER:	Not that I'm surprised. No, I expect it by now. Every time there's a murder within ten blocks of this house, I look for Mr. Goodwin here lurking behind a garbage can.
ARCHIE:	I don't lurk, Inspector, and especially not behind garbage cans.
CRAMER:	You'll clown on the hot seat, Goodwin. And *you*, Wolfe! When I first found that Carolyn Endor came to see you—
ARCHIE:	Of course you were having her followed, she being indicted and all—
CRAMER:	—when I first found out, I said, "What the hell!" I mean, you have to eat, too.
WOLFE:	Deftly put, sir.
CRAMER:	But this! The same day! Don't try to tell me this is some kind of coincidence!
WOLFE:	Of course it isn't a coincidence.
CRAMER:	By God! You admit it!
WOLFE:	Mr. Cramer, we know each other. Am I a witling? Are you? By no stretch of the imagination could I hope to convince you of such a palpable absurdity, nor would I try. Now as you have connected the man killed on my doorstep with Miss Endor, I am within my rights in asking two questions. First, did *she* kill him?
CRAMER:	No. My man says she never left her apartment this evening.

WOLFE:	Thank you. Second, who is the victim?
CRAMER:	You mean you don't know?
WOLFE:	I have a strong surmise. Will you confirm it?
CRAMER:	Let's hear it.
WOLFE:	I do not know what name he has assumed, but he was once known as Guy Angleton.
CRAMER:	Yes. You've got it. Now I'll ask you one. Who killed him?
WOLFE:	I could tell you.
CRAMER:	What!!?
WOLFE:	But I might be wrong. I expect confirmation in a day or two.
CRAMER:	Confirmation be damned! You'll tell me now!
WOLFE:	Confound it, no! It is futile, Mr. Cramer, and you know it. I will tell you in my own time or not at all.
CRAMER:	By God, Wolfe, I—
WOLFE:	Would it influence you if I were to tell you that Mr. Stahl of the FBI was in this office not half an hour ago?
CRAMER:	Stahl! What did he want?
WOLFE:	He wanted me to drop my investigation. Naturally I refused. By your reaction, I gather that he has been in contact with your department.
CRAMER:	Officious little—
WOLFE:	Precisely. I ask for two days, Mr. Cramer. I shall deliver the murderer to you before Mr. Stahl has an opportunity to exercise his authority.

CRAMER:	Yeah? and why would you do this for *me*?
WOLFE:	Do you wish me to be sentimental? Then it is because of my esteem for you. Do you wish to be cynical? It is because I find your demeanor less repugnant than Mr. Stahl's.
CRAMER:	You had better have it, Wolfe. Two days.
ARCHIE:	I showed Cramer to the door. The lab boys were finished and the wagon took Angleton away. I went back to the office. Wolfe was leaning back in his chair, his eyes closed. "Well, you've solved it."
WOLFE:	No.
ARCHIE:	You know who killed Angleton.
WOLFE:	Yes.
ARCHIE:	And Mordred.
WOLFE:	Yes.
ARCHIE:	But you haven't solved it?
WOLFE:	No.
ARCHIE:	How did you know it was Angleton?
WOLFE:	Who else could it have been?
ARCHIE:	I see. You know, sir, I never really appreciated your genius until now. That's neat.
WOLFE:	I am not being facetious, Archie. Mr. Angleton was a recurring and—until one hour ago—a missing factor in this problem. An unknown man being murdered on our doorstep was too dramatic an event to be fortuitous. Therefore I formed a conjecture as to his identity and, as you saw, it was confirmed.

ARCHIE:	And the identity of the guy who bumped him off?
WOLFE:	Archie, I am hungry. I cannot think when I am hungry. Shall we go in? Fritz has prepared an impromptu meal as the filets of beef—
ARCHIE:	And that was that. He didn't say another word about the case for the rest of the night. After my full eight hours, I came down to breakfast. Half of my mind was on the case, half was on whether I could still dance the tango and half was thinking up a fit punishment for Wolfe for not telling me what was going on. I decided a crazed Harvard alumnus was killing the Yale class of 1979 because they won the big game, a conga line would do and a first step might be to lure Wolfe to a fast food joint and chain him to the counter when it occurred to me that no one has three halves of a mind. Wolfe thinks he has one and a quarter—and he may be right— but not one and a half. I was starting my first griddle cake when— *(Buzzer)* The house phone buzzed and I picked up.
WOLFE:	Archie, this is intolerable. I know what was done and how it was done and who did it, but not why. I am told that syndicated radio programs are preserved on tape. Get me the tapes of Robert Rotterdam's past three or four broadcasts. I must hear them.
ARCHIE:	If you're thinking of defecting to the Soviet Union, I'm certain I—
WOLFE:	Archie! Even in jest—get me those tapes.
ARCHIE:	Yes, sir.
WOLFE:	But first go up to the plant rooms. Theodore has two *laelia purpurata* prepared and packaged.

	See that they are delivered this morning to Miss Endor.
ARCHIE:	Now he was sending her flowers. Well, sir, allow me to be the first to congratulate you.
WOLFE:	Congratulate me?
ARCHIE:	On your upcoming marriage. I hope you and Miss Endor will be very happy and—he hung up. Having no one to talk to any more, I decided to go up to the plant rooms where Theodore was getting ready for his morning session with Wolfe.
THEODORE:	Good morning, Archie.
ARCHIE:	Good morning, Theodore. You have a package for Mr. Wolfe's fiancée?
THEODORE:	His—what?!!
ARCHIE:	His fiancée. The woman he brought up here yesterday. He's going to marry her and lose one hundred pounds and move to a cottage in the country.
THEODORE:	With her?
ARCHIE:	Of course. There'll be room once he loses the weight.
THEODORE:	No, I mean with *her*? Does Mr. Panzer know about this?
ARCHIE:	Mr. Panzer? Saul Panzer? Why should he care?
THEODORE:	Well, he is her father. If Mr. Wolfe is going to—
ARCHIE:	Wait. Wait a minute. Wait. *(He pauses)* Wait.
THEODORE:	Yes?
ARCHIE:	Saul Panzer. Carolyn Endor. Father. Daughter.

THEODORE:	Yes.
ARCHIE:	Are you sure?
THEODORE:	Oh, yes. Mr. Wolfe mentioned it when he was up here with her yesterday and—
ARCHIE:	But I wasn't listening any more. I was on my way to the house phone. I should have counted to ten, but I wasn't thinking any more, either.
WOLFE:	*(Filtered)* Yes.
ARCHIE:	All right. I'm used to you not telling me things, but this is the limit. Why didn't you tell me that Carolyn Endor is Saul's daughter?
WOLFE:	Why, Archie, surely you know that my faith in your tremendous memory is boundless. I was certain that you would recall Saul has divorced and his wife got custody of their child and that their child's name is Carolyn and that his wife's maiden name is Endor—
ARCHIE:	All right! I won't ask for pity because pity is illegal, immoral and fattening, but—
WOLFE:	We shall say no more about it. The state of tension in this household of late has been disruptive. Hostilities will cease immediately. Agreed?
ARCHIE:	Agreed. That's me. Archie Agreeable—
WOLFE:	Archie?
ARCHIE:	Yes?
WOLFE:	The flowers and the tapes?
ARCHIE:	So I went. After calling a messenger, I went to WCBJ, chatted with Mary Kindel and brought the tapes home. I set up the old tape recorder in the office after Wolfe came down from the plant

rooms. Wolfe reached for his book, looked at the machine, pulled his book to him, looked at the machine, opened the book, looked at the machine, closed the book and sighed.

WOLFE: Archie, you will please show Fritz how to operate that device. Then you will get me Senator Bugatto and Robert Rotterdam. I shall be speaking to Saul and he will bring Miss Endor. I would like them at nine this evening.

ARCHIE: I wish I could say that obtaining the presence of a senator in the middle of a campaign and a lawyer whose time was booked a year in advance took a mighty effort on my part. Actually, Lily Rowan is one of the senator's closest friends and largest fundraiser and once we had Bernie—as I was told to call her—getting the counsellor was a snap. Since I didn't want Wolfe to know that, I had lunch with Lily and walked back to the office, arriving at about three. Wolfe was sitting in his chair staring into space. Fritz had just started a tape and was leaving to resume work on dinner.

KINDEL: *(Filtered)* Robert Rotterdam Reports to the People, July 24, 1984, Number 43. *(Pause)* It is with great pride and pleasure that I introduce noted civil rights attorney Robert Rotterdam with his latest report to the people.

ROTTERDAM: *(Filtered)* Thank you, Ms. Kindel. My letter today is from the *New York 5*. They write to ask whether today's exploitation is a subject for pity or blame on the part of the suffering masses. The answer, the only answer, is blame, *New York 5*. Yes, blame the exploiters for suffering, for pain, for agony. Blame them for suffering in any form until social justice makes all people happy. Blame them and blame them again. Yes,

New York 5, there must be no pity. *(Pause)* My report tonight is about the quagmire in Central America, where … *(He fades out)*

ARCHIE:

I've heard that speech end, so the thrill was gone. I went to the kitchen for a glass of milk and to see if I could help Fritz. I couldn't. He was preparing chestnut soup, lamb cutlets, squash, mushrooms, devil's rain dressing and apples baked in white wine and the real work, shelling the chestnuts, had been done the night before. When the half hour was almost up, I returned to the office. Rotterdam ended as he did at the studio. I turned off the machine. Wolfe leaned back and started his lips in and out. I knew that furious exertion meant that he was working full steam. One time he went on for— but you'd think I was boasting on his behalf. Actually, it only took seventeen minutes by my watch before he stopped working his lips and turned to me.

WOLFE:

Archie, Saul and Carolyn Endor are getting to know each other, but Saul does not feel it would be proper for him to invite her tonight. You must get her.

ARCHIE:

Just like the fat fraud. Assume I can rustle up senators and attorneys at will and send me away when things were getting interesting.

WOLFE:

Oh, yes, and dial Inspector Cramer for me. *(A pause)* Mr. Cramer? Nero Wolfe. I told you that I might have something for you tonight. It is now a certainty. (You may go, Archie.) You have searched Angleton's apartment? There was what? I see. Then please apply for another search warrant and an arrest warrant in the name of … Go, Archie!

ARCHIE:

So the hostilities are over, huh? But I went.

✗ ✗ ✗ ✗

ARCHIE: Compared with some of the scenes Wolfe has
            staged, this was fairly simple. Carolyn Endor
            was in the red leather chair, all the yellow chairs
            were placed so that I could get a good view.
            Like feuding actresses, Cramer and Stahl sat at
            opposite ends of the room. (I don't know how
            Stahl knew to come. Wolfe didn't invite him and
            he certainly didn't find out from Cramer. I de-
            cided I'd better check the office later for bugs.)
            In the back, Purley Stebbins and some uniforms
            watched the door and pointedly ignored Saul
            Panzer, who was on the sofa. No one wanted
            refreshments. At precisely nine o'clock Wolfe
            entered and sat behind his desk. Immediately
            the show began.

(ROTTERDAM, BUGATTO and STAHL speak at the same time.)

ROTTERDAM: I object most strongly to these proceedings.
            Miss Endor violated my strict instruction!

BUGATTO: I hope you realize I cancelled an important en-
            gagement to be here.

STAHL: Mr. Wolfe, you are jeopardizing an operation of
            the utmost importance.

WOLFE: *(Loudly)* Ladies and gentlemen! Intolerable as
            these inconveniences may appear, the acts of
            murder, treason and espionage are more intoler-
            able still.

ROTTERDAM: If you think to accuse one of us of those crimes,
            you had better be prepared to face legal action.

WOLFE: The prospect does not deter me, Mr. Rotterdam.
            Interruptions, however, both annoy me and de-
            lay the inevitable resolution of this situation. I
            must ask you for no further interruptions.

ARCHIE:	No one was overjoyed, but they did sit down again. I wonder if they have a class at Yale on springing to your feet. Buggato and Rotterdam both beat Stahl by an easy half-second.
WOLFE:	First, some history. Miss Endor, Mr. Mordred and Mr. Angleton knew each other at Yale, which Senator Bugatto earlier attended along with Mr. Rotterdam. Mr. Rotterdam was an early and important supporter of the senator's first campaign. Miss Endor, Mr. Mordred and Mr. Angleton worked on that campaign. Within six months of Senator Bugatto's election, Angleton disappeared, Mordred repudiated his leftist political opinions and Rotterdam was repudiated by the senator. Patently that first campaign was a catalyst of some sort.
BUGATTO:	That charge is the sort of gutter politics that my opponent—
WOLFE:	Senator I am not above politicking, but I reserve the practice for less serious occasions.
ARCHIE:	She sat. Apparently I could quote that.
WOLFE:	Now some facts. You all know that Guy Angleton was killed on my doorstep within the past thirty hours. You may know that Mr. Angleton was a member of the terrorist organization Liberation. But only two of you—Mr. Stahl and the murderer—knew that Mr. Angleton was actually infiltrating Liberation for the FBI.
STAHL:	Mr. Wolfe!
WOLFE:	Please, Mr. Stahl, no interruptions.
STAHL:	I wish to confer with you.
WOLFE:	No, sir! We shall confer afterwards if you still think it necessary. Please sit down. In

considering the details of this history, we confront some apparent paradoxes. Why did a radical extremist participate peacefully in a legitimate major-party political campaign and within six months take part in an assassination and turn fugitive? The paradoxical element here is not the assassination and the flight, but the campaign. Again, why did another radical extremist also take part in the campaign and then become a reactionary extremist? If, however, Mr. Angleton's terrorism and Mr. Mordred's reactionary conversion are in reality similar, it is because of their exposure to the one person who is present throughout this case, Robert Rotterdam. Sit down, sir.

ROTTERDAM: You can't silence me, Wolfe.

WOLFE: Obviously. But you cannot deny that you have had an influence on the destinies of everyone concerned in this affair.

ROTTERDAM: What are you saying, Wolfe? Remember you have witnesses.

WOLFE: Indeed. I prefer that all of my dealings remain open and aboveboard.

ROTTERDAM: This witch hunt has gone on long enough.

WOLFE: No. A little longer. At this point in my thinking, Mr. Rotterdam's involvement was merely suggestive. Any guilt on his part needed corroboration. That arrived this morning. I would like to introduce to those of you who do not know him, Saul Panzer, an operative whom I have had occasion to employ. He is Miss Endor's father. Saul?

SAUL: I should probably explain that when Carolyn went away to Yale on a scholarship, her mother and I were separated. Carolyn did not think Panzer would be an appropriate name for someone in the radical movement and when her mother died, she adopted my wife's maiden name. Carolyn always was headstrong and she made it clear when I told her my opinion of engaging in radical politics—and my opinion of Ashley Mordred—that she didn't want to hear from me. I obeyed her request, but I did keep in touch with friends in New Haven and later in New York who knew her. I was happy when she came to New York for Senator Bugatto's campaign, even if she was still infatuated with Mordred. A few months later, I heard she had broken with Mordred and taken up with Robert Rotterdam. Then Mordred announced his conversion. I was concerned, so I asked my friends some questions. It seems that all the events were related. My friends thought they had an emotional connection, but I do not know about that. In March, Ashley Mordred broke with the Left and Carolyn started seeing Robert Rotterdam. The assassination was in April. My friends in the radical movement did not believe Mordred's conversion and I believe them.

WOLFE: There are historical parallels. Several of the British spies recruited at Cambridge were instructed to renounce their leftist beliefs and assume the guise of fascists.

SAUL: Do you want me to go on, Mr. Wolfe?

WOLFE: No, Saul, we should reserve something. These facts are merely indicative, but they were enough for me to act. I asked Mr. Goodwin to obtain tapes of Mr. Rotterdam's radio diatribes.

STAHL:	The station would not let us have them and we are forbidden under current guidelines to make tapes ourselves.
WOLFE:	And I am sure you always obey the guidelines. Mr. Goodwin tells me that it was in the manner of your "request" for the tapes that led to the station's obdurance.
ARCHIE:	I wonder if Mary Kindel knows the word obdurance. It's not quite how I reported her comments on the FBI to Wolfe.
WOLFE:	The tapes, of course, contain a code for the guidance of terrorists around the country. Their artificiality told me that. The key is counting words. In the program to be broadcast tomorrow night, for example, Mr. Rotterdam reads a letter purporting to be from the *New York 5*, you will count five words. In the answer, he says the answer is blame. That means you start listening when you heard the word blame. He says the key is pain, suffering, agony and the like. That means you count from every synonym for pain. He says things will end with happiness. That tells you when to stop listening.
STAHL:	What was the message in the broadcast?
WOLFE:	I find it difficult to believe that no one in the FBI has taped Mr. Rotterdam's broadcasts, perhaps as keepsakes. Nevertheless, I am sure that Mr. Goodwin can satisfy your curiosity later.
ARCHIE:	I couldn't read Rotterdam's expression—probably another Yalie trick, but I did notice the uniforms and Purley had taken positions to block his escape.
WOLFE:	Perhaps the most interesting aspect of this problem is the Angleton tape. Mr. Rotterdam read

a letter from Angleton while he was in hiding, but the tape contains absolutely no clues or instructions. It is as if Mr. Rotterdam wanted it to be analyzed. Mr. Stahl, did Angleton send that letter?

STAHL:

No, he always wondered why that happened.

WOLFE:

A carefully conceived blind. In summation, then, Rotterdam recruited Angleton and Mordred for purposes of espionage. He sent out Mr. Angleton on a rampage of terrorism and took particular care to avoid association with him. He had Mr. Mordred adopt what the spy writers call deep cover until such time as he was needed. I suspect he thought he could control a senator by using evidence of her radical past. I also suspect he thought Miss Endor was so infatuated with him that she would betray her trust on the senator's staff.

CRAMER:

The murders, Wolfe, get on with it.

WOLFE:

Mr. Panzer accompanied the police this afternoon when they searched Mr. Rotterdam's apartment under a valid warrant in his absence. He also inspected what was found in Ashley Mordred's apartment during the investigation of his murder. Among the photographs of Miss Endor during her radical days in the company of Mr. Mordred and Mr. Angleton that Mr. Mordred's newspaper had been assembling as part of its campaign against Senator Bugatto were some taken in front of the Shubert Theatre in New Haven that showed Robert Rotterdam speaking with the three of them. Since the theatre marquee would show the date of these conversations, they could prove that Mordred was still associating with radicals after his

	conversion. That is why Mordred took over the newspaper smear. It is also why he died.
CRAMER:	What do you mean? There were no photographs of Rotterdam in Mordred's apartment.
WOLFE:	Exactly. But your officers and Saul Panzer found some from the same collection in Mr. Rotterdam's apartment this afternoon. What happened to Ashley Mordred's apartment was this. He told Mr. Rotterdam the photographs existed. Whatever Mordred's motivation in doing so—and his lack of preparation argues that they were innocent—Rotterdam feared he would be blackmailed or exposed. He rushed to Mordred's apartment, killed him, planted evidence incriminating Miss Endor and took the photographs. There must be meetings canceled, microscopic traces of his presence, all the evidence that Mr. Cramer's men can and will find now that they know where to look.
ARCHIE:	Rotterdam hadn't moved. The way Cramer and Purley were staring at him, I expected whiffs of smoke to come from his head.
BUGATTO:	How did you know that Angleton was with the FBI?
WOLFE:	What was he doing on my doorstep? If he was not coming to see me and why would he be? —then he was coming to see Mr. Stahl and how else would he know where Mr. Stahl could be found? The information he had must have been very important to make him jeopardize his cover by coming out of seclusion. Evidence of Mr. Rotterdam's treason springs to mind. Rotterdam found out, followed Angleton here and killed him. Once again evidence can be found. If you look—

(The sound of a chair being knocked over and a struggle.)

ARCHIE: Rotterdam must have been pretty desperate to go for Wolfe like that, knowing he wouldn't get two feet. Purley and some cops were right there and on him. But at least he wasn't talking.

STAHL: Mr. Wolfe, I have to use your phone. I have to get a federal warrant.

WOLFE: I think not, Mr. Stahl. Mr. Cramer?

CRAMER: Robert Rotterdam, I have a warrant for your arrest on the charge of premeditated murder. Purley, take him out and read him his rights.

ROTTERDAM: I know them.

CRAMER: But we don't want any complaints, do we? Take him out.

STAHL: Cramer, he's wanted for treason and for killing a federal agent.

CRAMER: You can have him after the State of New York finishes with him.

ARCHIE: And that's how it stood. The case against Carolyn Endor was dropped, Senator Bugatto was able to turn her campaign around and Wolfe went back to the life of a cantankerous invalid. Then one day— "Mr. Wolfe, Lily Rowan is here."

WOLFE: Indeed. What may I do for you, Miss Rowan?

LILY: I have a message from Senator Bugatto, Mr. Wolfe. She wants to thank you for clearing Carolyn Endor.

WOLFE: The gesture is unnecessary but welcome. Is there anything else?

LILY: Just one more thing.

WOLFE:	What? What? Miss Rowan! What are you doing? Archie! Archie! What is she doing?
ARCHIE:	She's signing your cast.
WOLFE:	Archie! Stop her! Archie! ARRCHIEEE!!
ARCHIE:	I determined in the hall that Lily wasn't carrying any deadly weapons, so Wolfe was safe for the moment. It seemed a good time to go to the kitchen for a glass of milk and some gab with Fritz. So I went.

✗

The late Henry Enberg was a lawyer and an active member of The Wolfe Pack and the Baker Street Irregulars ("John Garrideb"), known for his wit and fiendishly difficult quizzes.

DEATH BY WATER

by Steve Liskow

Jenny Della Vecchia felt Charlie Hamilton's eyes undress her from clear across the lobby of the Wadsworth Athenaeum. She tolerated him because he married her college roommate, but now she felt more naked than the statues guarding the museum's entrance.

"Charlie." She twisted her face away so it remained the air kiss she intended. "I didn't get to talk to you at the funeral. My God, it was so sudden."

"Jenny." Charlie's voice felt more mechanical than ever. "Thank you."

His hands, cold as marble, pulled her close and she forced herself not to shiver.

"Careful," she said. "I'd hate to get paint on your suit." Charlie knew how to dress and marrying Lou meant he had enough money to do it. Surviving her meant he had enough to do it many times over.

"Paint," he said. "You're working on something?"

"I'm not good enough, Charlie. You know that." Jenny remembered Lou telling her she had the passion, but not the brush technique. As a curator, Lou was never nasty, but she was never wrong, either.

Charlie sagged like the sails on his yacht. "I still can't believe she's gone. I went down to Washington for that NEA funding meeting and I came back ...."

His eyes drifted into the recent past. "They think she fell getting into the tub. Hit her head on the faucet and drowned."

Jenny knew that Lou was only her own age, twenty-nine. This sucked hard.

Charlie used his presenting-a-financial-report-at-the-annual-meeting voice. "And she even told me before I left that one of her fortune tellers said beware of water. I warned her to stay away from the boat while I was gone, but I was just kidding."

His eyes slid down Jenny's legs. "I always said that stuff was bunk. Now I wonder."

In college, Lou carried a rabbit's foot, wore an ankh and followed enough rituals to exhaust an obsessive compulsive witch doctor. When she moved in with Jenny, she read her horoscope, cast the I Ching and asked Jenny to read her Tarot cards once a week. As Lou's bridesmaid, Jenny remembered watching her best friend conceal three different charms under her bridal gown. Six years ago seemed like a lifetime now. For Lou Hamilton, it was.

"Did all her psychics tell her that?" Jenny asked.

"I don't know. But whoever did, hit it right on the nose."

Jenny's boyfriend, Hartford detective Tracy "Trash" Hendrix, handled the case. He told Jenny enough so that her own ESP blared like HDTV, but Trash believed in the spirit world even less than Charlie did.

"Do you remember who her psychics were, Charlie?" she asked. "The ones she saw regularly?"

⚹　⚹　⚹　⚹

Sanford Lawrence's office on Wethersfield Avenue felt more like it housed an accountant than a psychic and the last time he read Louise Hamilton's horoscope he told her it was a good weekend to work on her tan.

Elzbietta Raskinova—Jenny couldn't miss the nasal "A" that meant she grew up around Norwich—had hair almost as blond as Jenny's, legs almost as good, and a wardrobe from Liz Claiborne. Her dialect distorted "Hamilton" into "Heimilton."

"Nothing in the numbers showed anything about water." Elzbietta was into numerology and Jenny hated math. "I told her it was a good week to be creative. I know she was looking at some new paintings for the Athenaeum." ("Aehtheneeum.")

Psychic Number Three, Lady Ramla, wore a headdress with gold coins across her forehead and a costume that reminded Jenny of every scarf her mother sold when she cleaned out their attic. A stuffed owl glared down from atop a hutch overflowing with candles, incense, a trumpet and decaying photographs. The furniture dated from the Golden Days of Radio.

"I knew you were coming," the woman told Jenny. Well, hey, she was supposed to be a psychic.

"Then you know why I'm here." Jenny knew shtick when she saw it. Her own father was a stage magician before he and her mother retired to Florida. She'd grown up helping with the mind-reading routine and knew the signals in how he worded a question before she wore her first training bra. By then, she could shuffle aces to the bottom of the deck and pick pockets with either hand, too. That was about the same time she realized that she knew who her science teacher would call on to answer a question before he did it. Then she discovered Tarot cards.

"I will answer all your questions." Lady Ramla had flawless olive skin. With her black hair down and less kohl on her eyes, even the sleaziest bars in Hartford would check her ID.

"When was the last time Lou consulted you?"

"Two weeks ago." The colors in Lady Ramla's headdress matched the throw on the couch. "I saw impending danger."

"How impending?" Jenny watched the woman's brown eyes avoid her own green ones.

"One does not set one's watch by the fates. It could have been from a few days to a few months."

Jenny felt her Bitch Alert vibrating. "What kind of danger?"

"I told her to be aware of water, but thought of boats or cruises. So sad. So beautiful."

"So rich," Jenny said. "Her husband stands to inherit about fifteen million dollars."

"You suspect foul play?" The woman's bracelets sent a soft susurration across the table.

"Lou was my best friend. She didn't drink or do drugs, so I'm wondering why she fell in a bathtub."

"I cannot help you." Lady Ramla's scarlet nails were long enough to pick locks.

Jenny pointed to the velvet mound on the table. "You can't look into your crystal ball and tell me what happened?"

"My vision comes from the cosmos and visits me unbidden. I can channel the forces for particular clients, but it has nothing to do with the crystal ball."

Jenny restrained an eye roll toward heaven. "Then why have it?"

"People believe what they wish to believe." Lady Ramla's bracelets whispered again. "My clients believe in Gypsies with crystals, so I give them their money's worth."

"Do you know Charles Hamilton?" Jenny asked. "Lou's husband?"

Lady Ramla stared at the covered crystal ball. "Louise told me he was a non-believer."

"He is." Jenny wondered why Lou even bothered to tell Charlie about Lady Ramla's prediction. And why he remembered it to mention to her.

✗   ✗   ✗   ✗

Tracy Hendrix—the guys in Major Crimes started calling him "Trash" when he got partnered with Jimmy Byrne—sat on Jenny's couch in jeans and a white shirt with the sleeves rolled up. She sat at the other end of the couch so he could play with her bare feet. It gave her chills, almost enough to counteract Hartford's July humidity, thick enough to chew. It was her night to cook and they were sipping a piquant little Chardonnay before the main course.

"Two of the three psychics never mentioned water," she said.

Trash put his glass on her coffee table and ran his fingernail along the sole of her foot. Even her hair shivered. "And the one who did mention the yacht, right? It doesn't mean anything, Jennikins."

The diffused sun through her skylight gave the whole room a romantic amber glow.

"There's something wrong, Trash. Trust me."

"There's nothing to go on." He massaged her arch and she fought back a moan. "The M.E. says the contusion on the back of her skull matches the faucets. The mat in the bathroom was a little bunched up, too, like she tripped getting into the tub."

"But—"

"I know, I know. You say she was really graceful, but mats do slip. Maybe she'd had a drink or two, we don't know. By the time her husband found her, she'd been dead at least thirty-six hours, plenty of time for any alcohol in her bloodstream to dissipate. And even if she wasn't drunk, he was in Washington, D.C., Thursday night when she fell."

"How do you know that's when she fell?" Jenny sat up and felt a drop of sweat roll between her shoulder blades. "Maybe Charlie killed her when he got home Saturday. Maybe he dumped her in hot water to make it look like she'd been there longer, you know, speed up decomposing?"

"I saw the body. She'd definitely been dead more than a few hours. Trust me." He reached for her foot again. "I like your green nail polish, by the way. Matches your eyes."

"And my belly button ring." She knew he was saving up for a diamond and she knew she'd say yes. She hadn't said no to him since the night they met. "But Charlie doesn't seem that upset."

"He's still in shock." Trash reached for his glass again. "Picture it, he comes back from a big funding meeting, finds his wife dead in the tub, what's he supposed to act like? And everyone shows grief differently. For all you know, he's cried himself to sleep every night for the last week."

"But he's going to inherit millions of dollars." Jenny went to the kitchen to get the dressing out of the fridge. She wore cut-offs because Trash thought her legs were one of her best features, or two, depending on how you counted. He loved her waist-length hair, too. When she wore it down, it hid two of his other favorites.

"Well, yeah." His voice floated around the corner. "Their wills name each other as beneficiaries, which is pretty common. Her lawyer told us the same thing and he was concerned, too. But it's straight as a plumb line."

He came up behind her and put his hands around her waist. "I know you don't like Charlie, but it's legit, honey. It's an accident, pure and simple."

"Trash, everyone's told you how superstitious Lou was, right?"

"Are you kidding? Everyone we talked to had at least one Lou Hamilton story. Rabbit's foot, tea leaves, you name it."

"So you know she always had to come into a room on her left foot?"

"Um, I don't remember that one."

Jenny turned to watch his eyes. "She stepped into a room on her left foot and looked to her left. Always. Don't ask me why, but she was already doing it when we roomed together in college. Classes, meetings, restaurants, movies, everywhere."

"Okay. But so what?"

Jenny took his hand. "Let me show you something."

When she switched on the bathroom light and pushed her shower curtain aside, he hesitated.

"Is this going to get kinky, I hope?"

"Only if you're good," she said. "Watch closely, now."

She stepped into the tub, left foot first.

"Aren't you going to take your clothes off?" She heard the disappointment in his voice.

"Not until after dinner. You're going to need your strength." She sat down in the tub, and he watched her metallic green toenails while she played with the faucets. She stood up and watched him frown, then bent forward. If her long hair weren't in a bun, it would cover the burnished taps in front of her.

"Um, do you always get into the tub that way?" he asked.

She knew he saw it. "Doesn't everyone? Don't you?"

"I usually take showers," he said. "But… yeah. Her tub faces the same way. She would have stepped into the tub with her left foot, too, wouldn't she?"

"Uh-huh. That way, she could lie back against the slanted end if she wanted to read. If she got in the other way, the faucets would poke her in the back."

His eyes moved to the fixtures again. "So if she fell, the faucets should have hit her in the face."

He chewed his lip. "He was in Washington, Jenny. Twenty people talked with him. His flight got back to Hartford at eleven Saturday morning."

Jenny let him help her out of the tub. "After we eat, I want to try something, okay?"

They shared a Mandarin orange and chicken salad that neither one tasted before she led him back to the living room and turned off all the lights except one.

"More atmosphere?" he asked.

"Um-hmm," she said. "Plus, I'm trying to seduce you."

"Oh. Okay."

She opened the drawer and found her Tarot cards wrapped in the red silk that had been a camisole in its past life. She would have worn it on her wedding night three years earlier, but she read her fiancé's cards two weeks before the ceremony and found out he was cheating.

She unfolded the silk and put the cards on the coffee table. "I use a name spread, so that might be enough to do what we need."

"Which is …?" He looked at the cards, then at her, cross-legged on the floor across from him. It felt warm in the room and she couldn't decide if it was the sun through the skylight or his eyes on her.

"A reading for Lou." She nodded at the deck. "Work with me, Trash Man. Shuffle the cards, the more the better, and say Lou's full name out loud while you do it. Then cut three piles on the table."

The pack had seventy-eight cards instead of fifty-two and they were slightly longer than normal playing cards.

"Louise Lathrop Hamilton. Louise Lathrop Hamilton." Trash said it ten times while he shuffled. He shuffled awkwardly, but Jenny didn't want to handle the cards and influence their message. When he finished, she guided him through dealing the name layout on the coffee table. She repeated Lou's name while he did that, too.

Her eyes sank into the three rows: six cards, seven cards, and eight cards, corresponding to the letters in Lou's full name. The room felt even warmer and the pictures on the cards pulled her into them, the vibe so strong she could hear them shrieking.

"For broad influences in her future, I see power used for destructive ends—the Magician inverted—and betrayal or a family quarrel."

"That's the ten of … cups?" he asked.

"Right." The pictures on the cards shimmered when she looked at them. "And look at the second card in the second row, the Page of Swords. That's the twenty-ninth card, the same as her age, so it's really important. It can mean a surprise or illness. Or maybe an imposter likely to be defeated."

"Who could impersonate her husband?" His foot tapped on the floor, which meant he was excited, even if he didn't admit it.

She touched the center card in the second row. "The King of Pentacles. Charley's dark. And upside down, it can mean misusing your talents. And there are dark women all over the place. The Queen of Pentacles, the Queen of Swords, the Empress upside down. But Lou was blond."

"How about this one?" Trash pointed to the King of Wands, corresponding to the "L" in "Hamilton."

"A blond, blue-eyed man." Thinking about the dark woman triggered her Bitch Alarm again. "No, wait a minute. Upside down, it can be advice or a quarrel. And it's in the spot that means her immediate future."

The lamp spilled a pool of light in the otherwise dark room. "The Emperor upside down can mean injury, too."

She forced herself to look up and break the spell.

He wasn't smiling now. "Can we deal them out again?"

She wiped the cards with her red silk and watched him re-shuffle. This time, a treacherous woman with dark hair showed up three times. A surprise attack appeared twice. The Six of Swords, journey by water, indicated Lou's present circumstances.

Trash's feet tapped out a heavy metal drum solo. "It's all bull."

"No." Jenny sank back and let the room stop whirling. "You agree with me about the faucet?"

He reached for her left foot again.

"But how can I prove it?"

His fingers slid between her toes and she bit her lip.

"Why don't we sleep on it?"

✗   ✗   ✗   ✗

When Jenny walked into Charlie's office the next morning, he still wore his suit jacket, a testament to the building's air conditioning in the sticky heat outside.

"Jenny." He came around the desk just as she hoped he would. This time, she let him grope her a little. It distracted him from her own hand rubbing his hip, then sliding away to her purse before she stepped back.

"Charlie. Are you sleeping all right?"

"I'm getting by." Actually, he looked pretty good. His cheeks glowed and those shifty eyes looked every bit as lecherous as she remembered.

She sat in the chair across from him and crossed her legs in the carefully chosen short skirt. "Charlie, a few of us were talking a day or two ago and we'd like to start some kind of program in Lou's name."

"A program?" His eyes moved from her legs to her face.

"Uh-huh." She should have had her hair down so she could play with it, but the humidity would have turned it to a blond dandelion before she got out of her car. "We haven't worked out any details yet, but we were thinking of something like ... oh, I don't even know. An endowment, or a scholarship, or something. You know, to perpetuate Lou's name. The Louise Lathrop Hamilton endowment. Or maybe an internship. You know a lot more about that kind of thing than we do, and I told them I'd toss the idea out and see if you'd help us run with it."

"Why, I ... well ... It sounds like a great idea. What kind of capitalization were you looking at?"

"Um ... does that mean up-front money?" Jenny blinked and crossed her legs the other way. "Like principal?"

"Right. You keep the principal intact, put it into a CD or something and just spend the interest. Obviously, this is a bad time for investing, but ...."

"Well, we didn't have a really concrete idea yet, Charlie. I just wanted to feel you out before we went too far. I mean, Lou was your wife."

Charlie's fingers stroked the Mont Blanc pen on his desk. "Why don't you give me a few days to think about it?"

"Of course." Jenny stood again. "I know this is a lot to spring on you all of a sudden. I'll pop back in when you've had a little time to think about it, okay?"

"Sure." Charlie stood again, his suit immaculate. Jenny reflected that Trash Hendrix always looked a little rumpled.

Jenny felt Charlie's eyes on her hips until she closed the door behind her and scooted to the ladies' room on the lower level. Once she was alone, she dug in her purse for Charlie's cell phone and scanned his address book. Sure enough, the name she expected popped up, a cell icon next to it.

Jenny slipped into a stall so she wouldn't be disturbed and chose the number. Then she texted what she hoped would look like a frantic message:

Cops on2 us smhw. Meet @ Cntntal R Lnes contr, Brdle, 2:15. Dnt cll bk.

She made sure the message went through, then erased it and turned off the ringer. Charlie's phone was only half the size of her

Tarot deck and it nestled cozily in her hand while she knocked on Charlie's door again.

"Charlie? I'm sorry, I forgot to mention a little while ago …."

She leaned over his desk and felt his eyes slide to the "V" in her blouse. "A few of us are going to be at Black-Eyed Sally's tomorrow night, tossing more ideas around. We'd love to see you."

She dropped his phone on the thick pile carpet, where it bounced silently and lay near his foot. He'd find it eventually, but not until she was gone.

✗　✗　✗　✗

Jenny felt Trash's eyes on her from across his small kitchen. They felt soft and warm, nothing like Charlie's bludgeoning leer, and his face spilled over with questions he clearly didn't want to ask.

The pan on his stove sizzled with his own special stir-fry recipe, heavy on the soy, which gave them both an excuse to sip the pinot grigio he'd picked up after calling her.

"It was the damnedest thing," he said. "I mean, what can I tell Byrne? My girlfriend's Tarot cards say Charlie offed her?"

He added more ginger and waited for the angry hiss, a cloud of steam appearing above the pan. He cooked pretty well for a guy, another reason he was a keeper.

"I'm typing up the report, Byrne's telling me to let it go and worry about the other cases we've already got on our plate, when the switchboard sends us up this anonymous tip."

Jenny guided her wine glass to her mouth with both hands. She'd called the main switchboard instead of Trash's cell because she couldn't afford to have him recognize her voice. She used the phone booth three blocks down on Asylum Avenue, too, instead of her cell.

"What was it?" She was getting a little buzz from the wine, but she remembered to play innocent.

"This caller told us that Charlie Hamilton and Elise Santiago— that's Lady Ramla's real name—were making a run for it and we could catch them at Bradley. We found the girl at the Continental Airlines counter waiting for Charlie. When we told her we were arresting him, too, she collapsed like a house of cards."

His apartment only had a window AC in the living room and bedroom. Fortunately, Jenny expected to have most of her clothes off before too much longer. His, too.

"So you arrested him?" She watched him wipe his forehead on his sleeve.

"He was still at his office. But the girl gave us enough to get a search warrant for both phones and they had each other's cell numbers."

In jeans, he had an Olympic-class butt, too. "He told us she killed Louise, which makes sense with his alibi. Then she said that he gave her the house key and the entry code for the alarm system. Which also makes sense. She waited until she saw Louise turn on the light in the bathroom, then she snuck in and caught her by surprise."

"But she pushed her the wrong way, so the bump was on the back of her head instead of her face, right?" Jenny hid her face in her wine glass.

"Yeah. He disarmed the alarm again and handled everything in the bathroom when he got home to mess up any fingerprints she might have left behind. She says he gave her a map of the house, too, but she burned it."

His eyes stayed on her for so long she knew he was waiting for her to say something.

"I wonder who that anonymous caller was." He refilled her glass. "Think your cards could tell us?"

"I didn't bring them with me." Sweat beaded her upper lip.

"Too bad." He slid the veggies onto plates and led the way to the dining room, the temperature dropping five degrees when they stepped into range of the living room AC.

He sat across from her. "After we eat, I was thinking we could try that bath tub reenactment again."

"I knew you were going to say that."

✗

Steve Liskow (www.steveliskow.com) is a former actor, theatrical director and English teacher whose short stories have earned an Edgar nomination and the Black Orchid Novella Award. *Blood on the Tracks* (2013) introduces Detroit PI Chris "Woody" Guthrie and draws on Steve's experience as a guitarist and DJ. The book won Honorable Mention for the Writer's Digest Self-Published Novel Awards in 2014.

GHOSTS OF THE PAST

by Laird Long

Charlie scooped up the giant pumpkin and gently tossed it into the back of the open trailer. He banged his massive arms with his huge hands, more from reflex than for warmth, like he used to do before a big boxing match. That much he remembered. Ten years ago a savage beating parked him in a state hospital for eleven months. The beating left his heavily-concussed brain with little memory of the past. But at six foot six, two-seventy, he quickly regained all of his former strength. 'Not much for brains, but goddamn for strong!,' is how his baba from the old country put it.

Charlie brushed dead leaves from his thick wool coat and let his eyes roam over the hushed snow-crusted countryside. It was the middle of October and thin blue smoke hung in the air. The air was crisp and chill and the gentle breeze carried a veiled, but friendly threat of winter. In the brilliance of the afternoon sun he could clearly make out his neighbor over a mile away in his own field. Orrie was working on his broken-down tractor, trying to pull one more year from the rusting hulk. Orrie still owed him a hundred bucks from the Super Bowl—Charlie had gone Bears, while Orrie crapped out on the Pats. Charlie was no homer when it came to money.

Charlie grunted contentedly, horked out a sticky yellow gob and bent down for another pumpkin. His mind held the thought of a hot cup of coffee and a cool wedge of pie—his wife always had something good waiting for him when he took his afternoon break. A rogue gust of cold air suddenly shoved him backwards, but he shrugged it off.

✗   ✗   ✗   ✗

One hour later, a long black Cadillac with out-of-state license plates steamed down the dirt road alongside Charlie's property. It was moving fast. It stirred up a whirlwind of dust and in Charlie's dented skull, a cloud of cobwebbed memories. He watched it thunder by like an unstoppable doomsday machine and then, not fully knowing why, he ran for the freshly-painted white frame house he called home. He anchored his huge body in the middle of the long driveway and his grim face signaled 'Stop!' The Caddie surged to a halt, its front bumper bouncing softly off Charlie's knees.

Four city men in funeral suits piled out of the car and fanned out in a skirmish line in front of Charlie. Three of the men gripped shotguns. The fourth spoke. "Long time, Paulie. Ten long years," he said. He was short, fat and oily. His stumpy brown teeth clenched a stumpy cigar and his hands were buried deep in his coat pockets.

"Don't know what you're talkin' about," Charlie said truthfully.

The pissed-on fireplug of a man coughed out a laugh and spat it into the dirt. "Yeah, yeah, I heard about the amnesia act." The dead cigar dropped from his mouth. The other men casually raised their weapons on cue. "We heard you didn't squawk. Couldn't. But the old man don't take no chances. So after ten years of witness protection bullshit, here we are—you know, to finish the job." The fat man gulped down some fresh air and broke into a coughing spasm; he was used to swallowing his air in chunks. He looked back at the scarecrow guarding the pumpkin patch, at the gently rolling hills beyond. "Quite a life you've carved out for yourself," he smirked.

"Life is where you find it," Charlie replied calmly.

The fat man nodded slowly, solemnly. "And death."

"Drop your guns now!" The voice seemed to thunder from the heavens.

The men spun around as a group at the sound, but they didn't drop their guns. The animatronic scarecrow with cameras for eyes and a speaker for a mouth stared down at them. It flailed its arms wildly. Charlie and Orrie put in ten months building the thing, but the kids and the customers loved it. It was operated by remote from Charlie's workshop in the house.

As the men gaped in astonishment at the cavorting scarecrow, Charlie's memory dredged up a few more things from his murky past. He went into action. He grabbed the man closest to him—a little guy with a scarred pimply face. He crushed the punk in his thick arms and fired the kid's shotgun, using a sausage-sized finger stuffed into the trigger guard over the little guy's broken digit. The gun boomed and one of the goons split open at the back. Shards of cloth and flesh flew into the air in a red mist. Charlie fired another blast. The gob in the longshoreman coat did a jig, folded up and plowed the ground with the side of his head.

The fat man ripped his hands out of his pockets and blazed away with a pair of .45's. The little guy caught in Charlie's love embrace jerked around a couple of times as the bullets tore up his insides and then noodled. Charlie shoved the body aside. The fat man ran for the field. Charlie opened up with the shotgun again. Fatso flew through the air and smashed to rest at the base of the scarecrow. The scarecrow went limp as Charlie's wife raced out of the house and down the driveway towards him. Her arms were outstretched and her face was soaked with tears of terror.

Charlie turned to meet her. The scarecrow looked on blindly as the fat man rolled over, squeezed off one more shot and then went cold. The heavy bullet tore through Charlie's thick neck. The only other witness to a certain prominent Teamster's disappearance toppled over and died in his wife's arms. He had forgotten one of the rules he used to live by: when your man is down, plant him; one more bullet—the final nail in the coffin. So the ghosts of the past stay buried.

✗

Laird Long: Big guy, sense of humor; pounds out fiction in all genres. Has appeared in many anthologies and mystery magazines and resides in Winnipeg, Canada.

STRIKEOUT

by Dan Andriacco

Aaron Champion paced his Astor House hotel room restlessly, puffing on a cigar and trying to come to grips with the magnitude of the looming disaster.

The Cincinnati Base Ball Club outbid other teams for top talent to assemble the finest squad that money could buy, the Cincinnati Red Stockings. Abandoning the flimsy pretense of amateurism under which their opponents pitched, caught and hit balls, the Cincinnati nine boldly proclaimed themselves the first professional base ball team. And Champion was the president of the club. Therein lay his problem.

With an eye-popping payroll, it would not be easy to deliver a return on their money to the hundreds of investors back in Cincinnati, young lawyers like Champion and other professionals with names such as Procter, Gamble and Longworth. Even though the highly-paid players had a better than fair chance at ending the 1869 season undefeated, the club was practically broke.

And now this! What the devil—

A knock on the door interrupted his thoughts. Champion permitted himself a faint ray of hope. Perhaps this was good news. He flung open the door. An unprepossessing man stood before him, stocky, below average height, with red hair and a wispy beard. Perhaps thirty years of age, he was slightly older than Champion. He looked as though he slept in his cheap suit.

"Oh," Champion said, bitterly disappointed. "I'm sorry, my good fellow, I have nothing to give you today."

"My name is Flannery, Mr. Champion. I write about base ball for *The Cincinnati Daily Gazette*." Judging by his accent, the newspaper didn't have a "No Irish Need Apply" policy.

Champion recoiled. A journalist not on his payroll! And an Irishman! He had been wrong to think the situation could get no worse. "What are you doing in New York?"

"*The Gazette* decided to follow the Red Stockings on their Eastern tour, now that the team has become such a sensation. I'm sure you know that the Gibson Hotel back home will be jammed tomorrow with two thousand people awaiting the results of the contest against the New York Mutuals."

"Yes, of course, but Mr. Miller of *The Commercial* is already traveling with us."

"Aye, and that's all the more reason for *The Gazette* to do so, Mr. Champion. After all, they are a competitor of ours. And your club is paying Harry Miller."

"And what is wrong with that?" The arrogance of the man! "It's a common enough practice."

"Oh, to be sure, to be sure. And well worth the investment, no doubt."

Without asking permission, Flannery squeezed through the half-open door. He gawked at the silk wallpaper and the deep carpets.

"What are you getting at?" Champion didn't try to keep the irritation out of his voice. He blew expensive cigar smoke in the Irishman's face to emphasize his displeasure.

"Well, the man who pays the piper calls the tune, doesn't he? I hear that Asa Brainard and George Wright are missing and there's not a word about *that* in Harry Miller's stories." He began to unwrap a cheap stogie.

"Missing? That's a lie," Champion lied.

"Is it now? I hear that Harry Wright is looking for his little brother and Brainard at this very minute. If he doesn't find them, the Red Stockings will be in a good deal of danger tomorrow. George Wright is the lynchpin of the team. He's the greatest player in base ball—everybody knows that."

And also the highest paid, Champion thought, mentally wincing at the shortstop's princely salary of $1,400 per annum.

"Mr. Flannery," he said aloud, "your speculations are quite—"

The door, which Flannery had not quite shut behind him, flew open with a bang.

"Aaron, I found them!" The bewhiskered newcomer was out of breath.

"Say no more, Harry!"

But Harry Wright, manager of the Red Stockings, ignored Champion. "They are under arrest in the city jail. And the charge is murder!"

✗   ✗   ✗   ✗

The jail on Centre Street in New York's Five Points area smelled foul and looked worse. *No wonder they call it the Tombs*, Champion thought. He felt humiliated walking toward the cells with a guard and Harry Wright. Harry had been a top-notch player himself, both at cricket and at base ball.

"I still cannot credit what happened, Harry," Champion said. "Our pitcher and our best batter charged with killing a woman of the streets!"

"Not exactly that. The victim was a woman of loose morals, as I understand it, but not a common prostitute. She was registered at the St. Nicholas Hotel just down the street from here. That's where she was killed."

Champion never heard of the St. Nicholas, but he knew that all the hostelries in this area were of the luxury class. "I suppose that's what comes of paying these players so much. They can afford the best of everything, even women."

The two men came at last to the cell where Asa Brainard and George Wright were imprisoned. George, a wiry man and slightly bowed legs, held on to the bars like a monkey in a cage. "Mr. Champion! Thank the Lord you've come to get us out!"

Champion shook his head mournfully. "I'm not here to get you out, George. No one can get you out. The judge is denying bail."

"But we'll miss the game!" Brainard cried.

"That might be my biggest worry, boys, but it shouldn't be yours, considering your situation."

George tightened his grip on the bars. "Harry, Mr. Champion, we didn't kill that woman. You've got to believe that!"

"We'd like to, brother," Harry said, "but consider the facts: The police received an anonymous note this morning with the name Florence Raymond and a room number at the St. Nicholas Hotel. It turned out to be her room. They found her there, strangled. Bruises on other parts of her body. You two, half-naked, passed out on the floor nearby."

"But only half," Brainard pointed out. "That's not so bad, is it?"

"Ma would be ashamed," Harry told his brother. "How did you ever get mixed up in a thing like this?"

George lowered his eyes. "I don't remember. I had a few drinks."

"More than a few," Brainard mumbled. "Both of us."

"Then how can you be sure you didn't kill this woman?" Champion demanded.

"We just wouldn't do a thing like that," George insisted, "drunk or sober."

"It could have happened in a fit of rage. Perhaps she spurned your advances."

Brainard gave a boyish grin. "Not very damned likely, that."

"Well, I'll do what I can for you boys," Champion said. "I can't practice law in this state, but I will secure for you the best available counsel." *Another outrageous expense!*

"They don't need a lawyer," his manager said. "They need a detective, someone to find the true killer. It's the only way we'll get them freed in time for the game tomorrow."

Champion laughed bitterly. "I'm afraid that would take more than just any detective, Harry. From the looks of things, it would take the likes of Allan Pinkerton himself!"

Harry nodded eagerly. "That's exactly who we need—Allan Pinkerton, king of the private detectives, the man who tamed the Reno Brothers and stopped a ring of assassins from killing President Lincoln before he even took office. He's in New York right now! I read it this morning in Mr. Greeley's newspaper, *The Tribune*."

Champion considered, hope warring with pessimism in his thoughts. "Mr. Pinkerton is an important man, and a busy one, I'm sure. Do you really think he would take on this sordid affair?"

"Do you really think we can afford not to ask him to?"

✗   ✗   ✗   ✗

Allan Pinkerton, who started life as a barrel-maker and a radical, was a powerfully built but not especially tall man of fifty. His firm handshake was delivered with rough hands. He wore a suit that didn't quite fit and his reddish beard needed a trim. But Pinkerton's hotel room at the Cosmopolitan Hotel, which had just reopened after a renovation and renaming, made Champion's quarters look a bit shopworn by comparison. He *must earn even more than my players*, the president of the Cincinnati Base Ball Club thought. *The cost to hire him will be ruinous.* Still, he had to try to engage the man's services for the sake of Asa and George—and the chance to beat the Mutuals.

"I don't very often handle cases personally these days, Mr. Champion." Pinkerton's soft burr, which his years in Chicago had not completely obliterated, betrayed his Glasgow origins. He regarded the younger man with searching blue eyes as they faced each other in hotel room chairs. "I have an entire army to do that—Pinkerton's National Detective Agency. You know our motto: 'We never sleep'."

Yes, everyone knew the motto and the image of the wide-open eye that accompanied it. That's why his detectives were known far and wide as "private eyes."

"With respect, Mr. Pinkerton, I don't need an army to prove my boys didn't commit this foul deed. I need Allan Pinkerton."

Pinkerton grunted. "I will not deny that I am intrigued. There is always a great deal of satisfaction in freeing an innocent man—if these men are indeed innocent. But I shall have to get the permission of the prosecutor first. That is one of Pinkerton's Principles: Never work for an accused criminal without the permission of the prosecutor."

"I'm sure that I admire your principles very much, sir. However, there's scarcely any time for that if we are to free George and Asa before tomorrow's match. And it's my understanding that the officials of this city—including the prosecutor—are in the pocket of a man named Tweed who would very much like to see the Cincinnatis defeated. Mr. Pinkerton, you are a man of the west. I hope your sympathies continue to lie in that direction."

"My sympathies lie with the cause of justice, Mr. Champion." As an abolitionist, Pinkerton put justice above the law as a matter time after time when he'd helped slaves along the Underground Railroad.

"In this case, the two are the same thing."

"That is far from obvious. To the contrary, the circumstances could hardly be more damning for your two base ball players."

Champion set his jaw. "I'll admit the case is strong, but it's not iron-clad. The clerk at the St. Nicholas admits he was gone for long periods last night. I have that from the city police themselves. Such absences would have permitted someone else to slip into the woman's room, kill her and sneak out again while George and Asa were dead drunk."

"You demonstrate perhaps more faith than practicality, Mr. Champion. But I admire faith, even though I am not myself a religious man." He smiled slightly. "And I have felt fondly toward your city ever since I made it my headquarters when we rousted the Reno Brothers from Indiana three years ago. All right, then, I shall look into this matter despite my reservations."

"Splendid, sir!"

"But I make no promises. If these two young saints of yours are guilty, there is nothing I can do to save their murderous necks."

"Oh, I would hardly call Asa Brainard a saint! He carouses, he stays up half the night, and he plays awful jokes on people. Many's the day that he's too sick to play and I know what kind of sick it is."

"And George Wright is something of a kindred spirit, I take it?"

"No, sir. He's a level-headed young man, normally. I'm sure Asa led him astray last night."

"Regardless of who did the leading, they wound up at the St. Nicholas Hotel. That is a rather elegant establishment. How could these boys afford to be keeping company with a woman who resided there?"

"They have money enough. George is the Cincinnati Base Ball Club's highest paid player—one thousand, four hundred dollars per annum. Asa is paid one thousand, one hundred dollars, just below the manager himself—that being Harry Wright, George's older brother."

Pinkerton's eyebrows shot up. "Those are handsome sums to be paying men who play at sport."

Champion sensed that the Scotsman was offended by the notion. "Indeed, sir," he hastened to agree, "but that is what it took to lure the best players from the Eastern teams."

"I must tell you that I recoil somewhat at the notion of a professional base ball team. To pay players debases the notion of sport."

"Perhaps so, but the fact is that most of the teams we play are professional—they just don't admit to it. We've tried to make this matter of salaries above-board to return honor to a game all too often besmirched by the involvement of gambling interests."

"But the cost—"

"It is backbreaking, there's no denying that. Our payroll this year comes to nine thousand, three hundred dollars and we have not yet turned a penny profit. I had to borrow three hundred dollars from the wife of one of our stockholders to finance this tour."

"But I understand that the tour has been a great success."

"In sporting terms, yes it has. Not a game lost in the seventeen outings since we left Porkopolis two weeks ago. Financially, however, it has been a disaster. The gate was but fifty dollars in Mansfield and eighty-one dollars in Cleveland. We need a strong showing in New York to boost the gate elsewhere in the East."

"Then this contest against the Mutuals is more than just another base ball game."

"Mr. Pinkerton, it would be no exaggeration to say that it means the very life or death of the Cincinnati Red Stockings. And without George and Asa in the game, it will be death for sure."

⚹　⚹　⚹　⚹

Less than an hour later, Allan Pinkerton and the two accused sportsmen were face to face on opposite sides of the cell bars.

"I am here to help you men," the detective said, "but I can only do that if you tell me the absolute truth."

"But we already told the truth," Brainard insisted. "We didn't kill that woman."

"I mean all of the truth. You cannot insist upon this story that you have forgotten who introduced you to Miss Raymond."

"We were drunk at the time," George said.

"Not too drunk to take off most of your clothes in Miss Raymond's room."

"We had help with that," Brainard said.

"So your memory is returning already! How remarkable."

George Wright winced. "Look, Mr. Pinkerton, Aaron Champion will kill us if he finds out the whole story."

"Would you rather that the hangman did the job?"

"It was Johnny Hatfield," Brainard said sullenly after a long silence. "He gave us the wench's hotel room number."

"He made sure she knew we were coming, too," George put in. "When we got there, the drinks were already set out and she was dressed for company—real friendly company, namely us."

"Who is this Johnny Hatfield?"

"The left-fielder," George said, as if astonished that the detective wouldn't know this. "He was with the Red Stockings last season, but he went over to the Mutuals for more money."

Pinkerton nodded. That money would undercut team loyalty didn't surprise him in the least. "I see. You did not mention his involvement to Champion because he would have been unhappy to know that you were consorting with a player on the other side."

"Worse than that," Brainard said glumly.

George explained: "Johnny left the Red Stockings under something of a cloud. It was never proved, but there were rumors that he was in league with the gamblers."

"Gamblers!"

"Is that important, Mr. Pinkerton?" George asked.

"Very much so. You have given me my first real hope that you may not hang."

✗ ✗ ✗ ✗

Pinkerton's trained hearing detected the footsteps running behind him on the street before he heard the shout. "Mr. Pinkerton! Mr. Pinkerton!"

The detective turned around. A stocky fellow with pale red hair stopped, put his hands on his upper thighs and bent over, panting.

"You are Mr. Allan Pinkerton, aren't you? The Chicago detective?" he gasped out in an Irish brogue with the rough edges smoothed over. He probably left the old sod as a child. Pinkerton himself had come to the United States as a young man already married.

"Do I know you?" Pinkerton asked. Always make the other fellow show his hand first.

"No, but it seems that I know you, doesn't it now? My name is Flannery of *The Cincinnati Daily Gazette*."

"Oh, a reporter. I am sorry, young man, but I never talk to reporters unless it suits my purposes."

"And just what is your purpose, Mr. Pinkerton? Why were you visiting Asa Brainard and George Wright in the city hoosegow just now?"

"I am not going to answer that question or any other." Pinkerton lifted his hat. "Good day, sir." He turned away.

"Well, it hardly takes an Allan Pinkerton to figure out what you're up to now, does it?" Flannery called after him. "Aaron Champion must have hired you to get his boys clear of that murder charge before tomorrow's game against the Mutuals."

Pinkerton faced the reporter. "I see that you know something about this affair, Flannery."

"I've just wired my account of the murder back to the *Gazette*."

"But it only happened this morning." He narrowed his eyes. "You could not possibly have gotten to New York by now even if you left immediately after the first word of the murder reached Cincinnati. You must have been here already."

"Aye, just like you. I came east to write about the Cincinnatis. Been hanging around them like a tick on a dog since they arrived in New York early yesterday. The murder was incidental to the sport as far as I'm concerned, you might say."

"You follow base ball, eh? Then tell me, Flannery, are the Red Stockings really that good?"

"No one can beat them—not if George Wright and Asa Brainard are in the game, anyway."

"Would you be willing to bet on that?"

"I already have. Just a few dollars, mind you. All I could spare on a reporter's pay."

Looking at Flannery's frayed coat, Pinkerton had no doubt of that. "The gambling on tomorrow's match is heavy, is it?"

"It would be hard to find a man with any sporting instinct at all who hasn't put his money where his heart is."

"So there is a lot of betting with the Cincinnatis favored to win. That presents a perfect opportunity for the gamblers to profit handsomely—if the Mutuals should triumph."

"But they won't! Unless—"

"Unless what?"

"Unless Wright and Brainard don't play! Saints preserve us! Do you think that was the reason for the murder of that poor woman— to knock those two out of the game?"

"I think it is highly likely. Come with me, Flannery. You may actually be useful. And if I am right, you will get quite a story before we are done."

"But where are we going, Mr. Pinkerton?"

"Out to the Union Grounds in Brooklyn. There is a certain member of the New York Mutuals who bears questioning."

✗　✗　✗　✗

"I understand you gentleman wanted to—" The tall lean man with the handlebar mustache stopped cold. "Say, I know you. Flannery, isn't it?"

"That's right, Hatfield. We used to talk now and then when you were with the Cincinnatis."

"Well, I'm not with the Cincinnatis any more and I don't rightly think I ought to be talking to you now."

"Your new allegiance did not stop you from talking to a couple of your old comrades on the Red Stockings yesterday, did it?" Pinkerton said sternly. "I understand you helped introduce Wright and Brainard to some of the, uh, finer sights of New York."

Johnny Hatfield turned his head and spit tobacco juice emphatically. "And who might you be, mate?"

"I might be anybody, but my name is Allan Pinkerton."

If the name meant anything to Hatfield, he didn't show it. "Well, if you're looking for companionship, that ain't in my regular line. I was just doing a favor for some friends. Old comrades of days gone by, like you said."

"It's the hangman you're doing a favor, more like," Flannery said.

"What kind of crazy talk is that?" Hatfield demanded.

"Are you telling us you have not heard what happened?" Pinkerton asked.

"Not if it has something to do with the hangman, I don't. What's this all about? Quit beating around the bush. Out with it!"

"Wright and Brainard are in the city jail," Flannery said.

Pinkerton looked Hatfield in the eyes, trying to get a read on the man. "They are charged with the murder of a woman named Florence Raymond ... a woman you introduced them to, or so they say."

"Oh, my sweet Lord!" Eyes wide open, jaw slack, Hatfield appeared to be surprised and shocked. "I only gave them her address and told them to look her up. I barely knew the wench, but still ... *Murdered!* Why'd they have to go and do a thing like that?"

"The police probably will say that it was a crime of passion committed under the influence of drink." Pinkerton spoke in an emotionless voice. "The accused men themselves, however, insist they are innocent."

"They would say that, wouldn't they?"

"I think there is an excellent chance that they are telling the truth ... and that Florence Raymond was murdered with the sole purpose of putting the Red Stockings's leading players behind bars and out of tomorrow's game. It was a setup—and you were a key player."

Perspiration formed on the base ball player's forehead. "No, no. It wasn't like that at all!"

"Then what was it like?" Flannery pressed.

Hatfield wiped his hands on his pants. "George and Asa were going to be kept out of the game, but not like that. The girl wasn't going to be hurt. They promised me that nobody would get hurt."

"They?" Pinkerton repeated. "You mean some gamblers who bet on the Mutuals?"

Hatfield paled. "Shhh. Quiet! You can't even say the word gam— You can't say that word around a base ball park. If even a whisper of this gets out, I could be ruined."

"Not as bad as Wright and Brainard—your old *friends*—are going to be ruined," Flannery spat. "But I guess friendship doesn't count for much when it comes to greenbacks. With all that money you're making just for tossing around a base ball, you still wanted more. You disgust me, you greedy bastard."

"It's not a matter of what I want any more, Flannery. I'm in too deep now. When certain people ask me to do favors, I have to go along whether I like it or not." A look of panic stole over his face. "Hey, I didn't say that. And if you say I said it, I'll deny it."

"And this time certain people asked you to—do what?" Pinkerton asked.

"Just tell the boys about this woman. I was to say that she was a friendly sort who liked the company of gentlemen like them—gentlemen with cash to spend."

"And then?"

"Well, last night was just to soften them up, to make sure they'd come back for more. Tonight she was going to guarantee they couldn't play in tomorrow's match—nothing permanent, you understand, just the worst hangovers they'd ever had."

"But something went wrong," Flannery said.

"Or else the woman's death was part of the plan all along," Pinkerton added.

"Even they wouldn't—"

"Who exactly are *they*, Hatfield?" Pinkerton spoke sharply, his Scottish burr thickening. "Name these gamblers."

The base ball player shook his head. "It's more than my life is worth to do that."

"If you let two innocent men hang and a woman's murder go unavenged, then your life isn't worth very much anyway. Where is your conscience, man?"

"I must have left it in Cincinnati or I never would have fallen under the influence of those bettors." He shook his head. "But I sure don't want Asa and George to hang if they didn't kill the woman."

"Then talk, damn it." Flannery appeared to be an inch from using fisticuffs to reinforce his demand. "Who was behind the plot against the Red Stockings?"

Hatfield sighed. "Well, that's a matter of judgment. I suppose you could take the blame all the way up to Boss Tweed himself, if you've a mind to—William Marcy Tweed, him who folks call the Grand Sachem of Tammany Hall. They say he elected Hoffman governor and picked Hall to be mayor. He runs everything in this town."

"And Tweed forced you to set up the Cincinnati players?" Pinkerton said.

"Ha, there's a laugh! Bill Tweed don't dirty his hands on anything like that. A man named Jake Garber came to me. He's the

Commissioner of Docks, which means he's part of the Tweed Ring. Only a handful of party men get to buy the big jobs like that."

"He's the one we have to get to, then," the detective said. "Where does he work?"

"Work?" Hatfield sounded incredulous. "He don't *work* anywhere. He just draws his salary. That's what makes it such a good job he had to pay ten thousand dollars and a share of the take to get it."

"He must do *something*," Flannery said.

"Sure—he drinks. There's one tavern he favors in particular—McGuire's. It's down by the docks, just a few blocks from the East River. Kind of a rowdy place."

⚡   ⚡   ⚡   ⚡

The crowd was noisy, the floor was covered with sawdust, and Pinkerton made it a point not to hold his tumbler of water up to the dim light. The detective, unlike most of his men, didn't drink alcohol or smoke.

"Yeah, I'm Garber." The Tammany Hall man was round with broken veins in his ruddy nose. He slurred his words when he talked. "If you're looking for a job, I don't have any right now."

"We have jobs, thank you." Pinkerton sat down and Flannery followed his lead. "My name is Pinkerton and I am a detective. This is Mr. Flannery; he is a newspaper reporter. We are inquiring into the death of Miss Florence Raymond."

Garber's puffy eyes misted up instantly. "Poor Flo! She was an old friend, you might say."

"You set her up to die." Pinkerton spoke coldly.

"Says who?" Garber's pugnacious attitude was almost comical, given the extreme unlikelihood that he could stand up, much less hold his own in a fight.

"Never mind that," Flannery said. "This is murder and you're in it up to your eyebrows."

"Your gambler friends had her killed, didn't they?" Pinkerton pressed.

"Hell, no! Where did you get that crazy idea?" Garber blinked his blurry eyes. "Everybody knows a couple of base ball players killed her."

"Then everybody is wrong," Pinkerton said.

"You forced Johnny Hatfield into sending Brainard and Wright to that woman, didn't you?" Flannery said. "It was a plot to seduce the Red Stockings's best players into missing the match with the Mutuals so that New York could win and the gamblers would make a bundle."

Garber downed half his glass of whiskey in one gulp. "You birds think you know everything, don't you?"

"Not everything," Pinkerton said. "Why did the men above you adopt such an uncertain plan? The whole scheme would have utterly failed from the start if the two ball players had proved immune to the lady's charms."

"They wouldn't have." Garber smiled "You didn't know Flo. Besides, my friends had no choice. They couldn't pay the players to lose the game on purpose—'hippodrooming' it's called. Harry Wright would have caught on and there would have been hell to pay."

"So they decided to eliminate the threat from George Wright and Asa Brainard by other means."

"Them two are lucky they're in jail. If they weren't, I'd murder 'em with my bare hands," Garber said. "Why the hell did they have to kill Flo, anyway? She never hurt nobody."

"We figure they didn't kill her," Flannery said. "We figure it was the gamblers, taking no chances that Wright and Brainard would be put out of action."

"If they were going to kill somebody, why not kill the two base ball players?" Garber objected.

"Because it could have been traced back to them too easily," Pinkerton said. "If they killed the Cincinnatis's top players just before the match with the Mutuals, the reason would have been obvious and the gambling element would have been suspect immediately."

"The bastards," Garber mumbled into his glass. "If that's true …"

"We'll make sure they pay, Garber, I promise you that. All you have to do is give us the names."

"Not a chance, Pinkerton!" He downed the last of his glass, which must have had many predecessors. "If they killed Flo like you say, they wouldn't stick at making sure I joined her right soon."

"We'll have the law on them before they can move against you."

"You don't understand. These people *are* the law. High up in Tammany. I'm naming no names."

"I'll bring in the federal marshals to take over this town," Pinkerton vowed. "I've done it before."

"I dunno, gents. I'm—I'm afraid." He signaled to a bartender who brought a fresh bottle of whisky and set it on the table, opened. Garber grabbed it and poured the dark liquid into his glass. His hand trembled.

"Telling us what you know may be your best insurance policy," Flannery argued. "As long as you don't tell, you're a threat to them—a threat they can eliminate with one blow. But once it's out, there's no need for them to kill you."

"Except revenge." Garber downed liquor. "And making me an example of what happens to anybody who crosses them. Those are reasons enough for Tammany Hall. But I'll think about it. I ain't easy about what happened to Flo. We had some good times together."

"You had better think fast," Pinkerton said. "Time is short. My job is to get Wright and Brainard out of jail by tomorrow."

Garber took another drink. He looked around the room and then leaned toward the other two men. He whispered loudly, as drunks are wont to do. "I'd best not talk here. The walls have ears. Meet me at the docks at the end of Eighty-Sixth Street in two hours. I'll tell you what you want to know."

⚡   ⚡   ⚡   ⚡

It was a foggy evening and chilly for June as Pinkerton and Flannery approached the place of rendezvous.

"What's that body of land over there, Pinkerton?" Flannery pointed. "It's too close to be the Jersey shore, isn't it?"

"That must be Blackwell's Island. There's a hospital for lunatics there, poor devils."

Flannery shuddered visibly. "Do you think Garber will show?"

"Time will tell. He could change his mind or fall in the river in a drunken stupor before he can get here."

But just then they heard the sound of footsteps on the wood of the dock.

"Garber!" Pinkerton called. "Is that you?"

"None other!"

Just as the Commissioner of Docks came into view, walking unsteadily toward Pinkerton and Flannery, three gunshots rang out in quick sequence. Garber fell into the water with a cry and a splash.

"Down, Flannery."

The little journalist dived behind a barrel. More gunshots followed, some of them fired by Pinkerton. When the hail of bullets stopped, the only sound in the mist was retreating footsteps.

"Damn!" Pinkerton swore. "They got away clean."

"What about Garber?"

"He never came back up. Nor will he, I fear. If the bullets didn't get him, the East River must have. Mr. Garber was right about his Tammany Hall friends. They didn't hesitate a bit about sending him to join his lady friend."

⚔ ⚔ ⚔ ⚔

Midnight found Aaron Champion discussing the day's developments in his room at the Astor with America's most famous detective.

"From what you've found out, Mr. Pinkerton, there can be little doubt that my boys were set up by the gamblers."

"None at all."

"Then they are in the clear and must soon be freed from that horrible jail!"

"Regrettably, that does not follow. First of all, there is the small matter of proof."

"But you have witnesses!"

"Not exactly. It is true that Hatfield and Garber both testified to me that gamblers wanted to get your two top players out of the way. But neither of them knew the killing of Florence Raymond to be part of the plot. Garber, who knew the most, is dead, anyway."

"But the involvement of gambling interests in base ball—"

"Does nothing whatever to absolve Wright and Brainard of the murder. And how will I ever prove that the gamblers *are* involved? Do you think Hatfield will talk after what they did to Garber?"

Champion slumped back in his chair. "Then we are undone."

"Perhaps not. There is still one hope for your men: a confession."

The attorney barely stirred. "From whom?"

"From you, Mr. Champion."

"What the devil!"

"You have admitted that the Cincinnati Base Ball Club is practically penniless. The Eastern tour is doing little to change that. Hundreds of investors are doomed to be disappointed, including many of your friends and some of the most respected names in the Queen City. Your status with them will be ruined, as will your pocketbook. But there would at least be money for you in tomorrow's match if you bet against your own team and then made sure that the best of the Red Stockings could not perform."

Champion sat in a silent fog of shock, anger and confusion for perhaps two minutes. Pinkerton didn't move a muscle, either.

"This is preposterous!" Champion stammered at last. "I have always hated the involvement of gamblers in sport!"

"All you had to do was prey on Asa Brainard's well-known habit of carousing. You could be pretty sure that he would pull George Wright into it and Miss Raymond's charms would do the rest. Maybe murder wasn't part of it at first, but someone finally realized the scheme was too chancy without it. That was probably the Tweed people—they supplied the girl. Yes, they would have told you what to do, reluctant though you might have been to do the deed."

"I don't even know any Tweed people!" Champion took a deep breath and forced himself to calm down. "This is absurd, Pinkerton—a fairy tale. You could never prove any of it."

"Indeed, I could not. It would take that confession *if your team is to have a hope tomorrow*."

Pinkerton smiled and the penny dropped for Champion. The detective wasn't making an accusation; he was offering a way out! It was a dangerous chance, but Champion saw no other. "And what would happen if I did confess?"

"Your players would go free. I am afraid that you would replace them in the Tombs until I can make a case against the true culprit. But it isn't you the Red Stockings need to win tomorrow's match, is it, Mr. Champion?"

✗　✗　✗　✗

The Red Stockings had a rough time of it the following afternoon, but managed to defeat the Mutuals 4-2 with two runs scored in the ninth inning. *The Cincinnati Daily Gazette* jubilantly reported: "We are tossing our hats tonight, and shaking each other by the hand. We are the lions, and base ball men are looking curiously at us as the club over whose grounds, it is possible, will soon float the whip pennant—emblem of the world championship … all this because we have beaten the Mutuals and because the game was the toughest, the closest, most brilliant, most exciting in base ball annals."

The morning after the game, Allan Pinkerton appeared at the train depot on Chambers Street just across from his hotel. He searched the crowds milling about until he spotted the man he sought, standing in line ready to board.

"Mr. Flannery!" he called. The journalist turned around. "I thought that was you. Are you going on with the team or heading back west?"

"It's back to Porkopolis for me, Mr. Pinkerton. I've had enough of base ball." He stretched his head, apparently looking for his train, then turned back to the detective. "Were you among the seven thousand at the match yesterday?"

"No, I was in my hotel room reading the copies of your stories that you gave me."

"I hope you found them enlightening, sir." His voice oozed Irish charm.

"Oh, very much so, especially your first story about Florence Raymond's murder. It was quite detailed. In fact, it included information about the unspeakable acts done to her body that was never made public."

Flannery smiled. "Not to boast, but that's what comes from learning how to get the coppers to talk."

Pinkerton shook his head. "No, that was your source of knowledge. In a corrupt system under the control of one man, discipline is very good. Tammany Hall controls Centre Street just like it does all the other levers of power in this godforsaken city. And Tammany has no brief for reporters who are not on the payroll. No one at the Tombs would have shared those gory specifics with you.

But, in point of fact, I have established that you never even showed up at Centre Street."

"I don't know what you're getting at, but I have a train to catch and it will be here any minute."

Indeed, Pinkerton could hear the sound of the locomotive in the distance.

"You did have one contact with the New York police," the detective went on, ignoring Flannery. "That was the note you sent them to make sure they found Florence Raymond's body before the two base ball players woke up. But you were equally helpful to the gambling interests—you tipped them to our meeting with Garber. Their killing him was supposed to make me all the surer that they and the Tweed Ring were behind Miss Raymond's murder. Instead, it made me suspect you, Flannery. No one else knew about our meeting with Garber at the docks. That's why I asked for copies of your story to see what you wrote."

"But it *was* gamblers behind the killing of that woman," Flannery sputtered. "Champion said so in his confession!"

"That must have seemed like an inexplicable gift from heaven to you, that confession! Or did you guess that it was a stratagem of mine for getting Wright and Brainard out of jail in time to play against the Mutuals?"

Flannery didn't answer the question as the sound of his train chugging toward the depot grew louder. "Why would I kill the girl? Not to get those base ball players out of action—I told you I bet on their team. I can prove it."

"I must admit that motive is the part that I am least sure about. But I know that you were closely following the Cincinnati players—you said as much. Perhaps you followed those two into Miss Raymond's room and killed her in drunken rage—no real reason at all."

"You have a lot of ideas, Pinkerton," the reporter snarled, "but not a bit of proof."

"I have more than you think. The police were so happy to find the killers they wanted that they didn't look any further. I did. A maid named Brigid Halloran told me that she saw a man matching your description leave Miss Raymond's room right around the time the murder must have taken place. I am confident that she will be able to identify you to the police."

"I wasn't drunk," Flannery said dully. "All right, I'd had a few drinks before I ran into Fred Waterman, the third baseman, and he told me where they'd gone. I was feeling good, but not drunk like Wright and Brainard. They were already passed out when I got there. So there was this fine-looking lady and me the only man in the room awake. What would you have done?"

"I would not have killed her."

Flannery raised his voice above the sound of the approaching train.

"I didn't plan on it, for God's sake. I attempted certain liberties, as the gentlefolk say. She laughed at me. *Laughed*. And I knew why. It was because I didn't have the fine clothes, didn't have the money. Not like her two gentlemen callers. Or maybe it was just a matter of 'No Irish Need Apply.' I lost control of myself once I had my hands on her. She was dead before I knew what I was doing."

"And you were perfectly happy to let two innocent men hang because you hated them for being well off."

Flannery's west-bound train loomed large now as it got close.

"The rich don't hang in this country, Pinkerton, only the poor. And those base ball players are rich as capitalists. I wasn't worried about them. But when you got on to the gamblers, I decided to let them take the blame. Why not? I really did have money on the Red Stockings, though I had little enough to risk and I would surely lose it if the boys couldn't play ball."

An immigrant himself and once a poor man, Pinkerton was not totally without sympathy for the Irishman. "You tell a good story, Flannery. Maybe you will only get prison time if the jury likes you enough."

"You'll not send me to prison. I couldn't stand that. I'd sooner die."

Heavier but younger than Pinkerton, the journalist began to run—but not to run away. He ran straight into the path of the massive locomotive pulling into the station. Pinkerton saw the panicked expression on the engineer's face or imagined that he could. The engineer hurriedly applied the brakes, creating an ear-searing screech, but it was too late.

Allan Pinkerton was a hard man, but not that hard. He turned his head.

Dan Andriacco, a long-time Sherlockian, is the author of *Baker Street Beat: An Eclectic Collection of Sherlockian Scribblings* and Holmes-themed mystery novels and collections. A frequent contributor to *SHMM*, Dan blogs at www.DanAndriacco.com.

THE COP WHO LIKED GILBERT AND SULLIVAN

by Robert Lopresti

When the phone call reached police headquarters no one was more surprised than Sergeant Emil Klinehart himself.

"Me?" He fumbled to turn off the CD player that had been filling the evidence room with the Lord Chancellor's song from *Iolanthe*. "They want *me* on a murder investigation?"

"That's what they said," said the desk clerk.

"But I haven't been out on half a dozen calls in the last five years. Why do they want *me*?"

"Who knows?" said the clerk cheerfully. "Maybe you're a suspect."

Five years ago, Klinehart rushed to investigate a missing child in a city park. He was in such a hurry that he forgot to set the handbrake on the patrol car. The little girl was found safe and sound, but it took a crane to pull the prowl car out of the fishing pond. Klinehart was banished to the evidence room as punishment.

Some punishment. He *loved* working alone, with his CD player blasting at full volume. Last year, following a scandal in the evidence room of a nearby city, a court-ordered audit declared Klinehart's to be the best-run room in the state. He had been promoted to sergeant and told to expect to stay there until he retired.

Now Klinehart was being pushed out of the nest, into the cold cruel world of real police work. He was not happy.

The address where the prowl car dropped him off was not reassuring.

The few homicides he saw as a beat cop had been in back alley tenements. This murder site, on the other hand, was an old mansion on the edge of the city.

A patrolman escorted him into the library, a room roughly the size of Klinehart's apartment. It was dominated by floor-to-ceiling bookcases and a huge antique desk at the far end.

There were two men in the room and the sergeant recognized one as Lieutenant Perez, reputedly the best detective on the force.

Why in the world would Perez ask for *him*?

The lieutenant smiled. "Klinehart, glad you're here. You're the guy who plays Gilbert and Sullivan recordings in the evidence room, right?"

He swallowed. "Yes, sir. If someone complained about the noise—"

"Nope." Perez shook his head. "We need an expert on Gilbert and Sullivan and you're the only one I know. Will you give us a hand?"

"Of course, sir." Klinehart's head was swimming. He had never heard of a Savoyard being needed for a murder investigation before.

"Lieutenant, may I ask a few questions?" The other person was speaking, a well-dressed man in his mid-fifties.

Perez nodded. "Sergeant, this is Alfred Edwards. He is the attorney for the man who was murdered last night." He waved a generous hand towards Klinehart. "Ask away, Mr. Edwards."

The lawyer fixed him with a doubtful look, as if Klinehart were a potential juror he was preparing to reject. "Have you noticed the statues, Sergeant? Take a look at them."

He hadn't spotted them until then. There were thirteen statues standing on wooden bases on a narrow table that ran most of the length of the room. Each was made of some sort of ceramic or clay and stood about a foot high. They appeared to have been made by the same artist.

Each portrayed a man in an elaborate costume. The first ones he picked out were two men in the robes and wigs of English judges and a Japanese man holding a huge axe. He began to get an idea of why Perez asked for him.

There were thirteen statues, but fourteen bases on the table. Edwards was standing near the empty base, the eleventh counting from the left side of the room, which Klinehart realized was the way to count them.

Edwards pointed to the empty shelf. "Can you tell us about the statue which used to stand there?" Klinehart glanced at the nearest neighbors of the empty shelf. On the left was a gentleman farmer. On the right stood a black-caped nobleman.

He let out a sigh of relief; if all the questions were this easy he would have no trouble. "It was a jester, sir."

Edwards's eyebrows went up. "Very good! Perhaps he *can* be of help, Lieutenant."

Perez was grinning. "How did you know, Sergeant?"

"The statues represent the Gilbert and Sullivan operas, sir. They show the Grossmith characters."

"The *what* characters?"

"Grossmith, sir. George Grossmith was the actor who played the main comic part in most of the original productions." He pointed to a few statues. "Koko from *The Mikado*. The ruler of the Queen's navy—" He pronounced it nay-*vee*. "From *Pinafore*. The only one missing is the jester from *The Yeomen of the Guard*. Did someone steal it?"

"No, we've taken it as evidence. The owner of this house was murdered last night. Apparently, he surprised someone in this room in the middle of the night. The prowler stabbed him with a letter opener from the desk."

Klinehart frowned. "Who was the owner, sir?"

"Jeremy Hollander," said the lawyer. "Let's start with some background, shall we? My late client spent many years in Hollywood as a character actor. He was never a star, but he worked steadily in character roles.

"He invested his money wisely and so, ten years ago when he reached fifty-five, he was able to retire and dedicate his time to his first love. Mr. Hollander was a Gilbert and Sullivan enthusiast."

"I've seen him," said Klinehart. "He performed with the Civic Light Opera in the Grossmith parts. I guess that's why he had the statues."

"Apparently," said Perez. "Now before he died Hollander struggled across the room and picked up the jester. We hope he was trying to identify the attacker. Of course it would have made more sense to go to the desk, but maybe he didn't think he had time to look for a pen and paper and it was farther away."

"But if it was a burglar—"

"It wasn't. The doors and windows were all secure. The alarm was set."

"I had to turn it off when I arrived this morning," said Edwards. "I flew all night to keep an appointment with Jeremy, and instead I discovered his body."

Perez nodded. "There are no servants here at night, so it appears that one of Hollander's four houseguests killed him. Last night was his birthday and all of his relatives were here to help celebrate. They are his nephew Douglas Anson, his grandchildren Stanley and Sally Long, and Stanley's wife Maureen."

He paused. "Do any of those names appear in the play?"

Klinehart shook his head. "I'm afraid not, sir."

The lieutenant sighed. "I suppose that would have been too easy. Well, let me tell you what we learned from the suspects' preliminary statements. Mr. Hollander took his guests out to dinner last night. During the meal he informed them that he had invited Mr. Edwards to come to the house in the morning, in order to finalize a change in his will.

"Apparently someone slipped into the library last night to get a look at the will, which was in the top desk drawer. Mr. Hollander surprised him—or her—and was killed."

Klinehart realized that he might never have a better chance to impress a Lieutenant. He wracked his brain for a good question. "What were the changes in the will, sir?"

The lawyer spoke. "Jeremy originally intended to leave the Civic Light Opera one-fourth of his estate. However, the group has fallen on hard times lately, so he decided to raise their share to one half. The rest is divided evenly between his two grandchildren and his nephew."

"Obviously they had a powerful motive," said Perez. "They knew that if he lived long enough to sign the will, they would receive a smaller inheritance."

Klinehart nodded. "And you hope the statue indicates the killer."

"It seems reasonable. Why did he stagger across the room to pick up a statue? Why that one in particular? Tell us the plot of the opera and maybe we'll get an idea."

The sergeant grimaced. "Gilbert's plots don't make much sense when they're condensed. To tell the truth, some of them aren't too clear at full length."

"We'll risk it," said Perez. "Just give us the highlights."

Klinehart took a deep breath. "All right. *The Yeomen of the Guard* takes place in Tudor England. The yeomen are the warders of the Tower of London, which is the play's setting. They're guarding a Colonel Fairfax, who was falsely accused of sorcery by his relatives and condemned to die."

"Are there any murders in the opera?"

Klinehart stared at the ceiling as he ran the plot through his head. "No, sir. There *is* an argument over a will."

"That sounds good. Tell us about it."

"Colonel Fairfax wants to get married in prison so that the relatives who framed him won't inherit his estate. A woman named Elsie Maynard agrees to marry him for fifty pounds, knowing that he'll be executed in a few hours."

"Fifty pounds," the lawyer repeated. "As his wife, wouldn't she get the colonel's entire estate?"

Klinehart shook his head. "I warned you this might not make much sense. We're never told who would get the rest of the money and since Fairfax lives happily ever after, it doesn't seem to matter much."

Edwards sighed. "Surely in Jeremy's final moments he wasn't thinking of anything so complex. If there is a clue it must be in a character's name or the title of the play."

"How about the jester?" asked Perez. "Does he have a name?"

"Jack Point, sir. Elsie was his fiancée and when he loses her he dies of a broken heart."

"Not exactly what killed Mr. Hollander."

"Sir," said Klinehart, "may I add something?"

"By all means, Sergeant. We called you down to get your opinion."

"Well, Jack Point is the only really tragic character in any of Gilbert and Sullivan's operas. If a comic actor *was* dying he might naturally be drawn to the jester with the broken heart."

Perez scowled. "You mean that Mr. Hollander might have picked up that statue for sentimental reasons that had nothing to do with the murder."

Klinehart nodded sadly.

The lieutenant shook his head. "For a while there I thought this would be an easy one. I guess we had better continue with the regular investigation. Why don't you take a seat, Sergeant. You'll probably enjoy the change after being stuck at headquarters for so long."

Actually there was nothing Klinehart wanted more than to return to the security of his evidence room, but it didn't seem advisable to say so. He sat down.

Perez ordered a patrolman to escort Sally Long into the library. "According to the preliminary reports, she has been the least cooperative," he explained to Edwards and the sergeant.

The first suspect to walk in, however, was certainly not Sally Long. He was a good-looking man in his mid-thirties and his casual clothes cost more than both of Klinehart's civilian suits together. "I'm Stanley Long, Lieutenant. I know you asked for my sister, but she locked herself in her room and says she won't come out until her lawyer arrives."

"You can tell her that Mr. Edwards is right here."

"Uh, Lieutenant." The attorney looked uncomfortable. "I told all the houseguests that as the executor of Mr. Hollander's will. I can't represent any of them."

Perez glared at him. "Oh, you did."

"I had to. Professional ethics."

The lieutenant turned back to Long. "Has your sister called a lawyer?"

"To be honest, I don't think she knows one, except for Mr. Edwards here." Long smiled wryly. "Sally is a painter, you know. She prides herself on her artistic eccentricity."

Perez heaved a sigh. "Well, let's start with you then, Mr. Long."

"Fine with me, Lieutenant, but I really don't know what you can ask that the first officer on the scene didn't."

"Oh, there's always another question. For instance, who do you think killed your grandfather?"

The next hour was a liberal education for Klinehart, his first chance to watch an expert investigator at work. As the questioning went on, however, he recognized that Perez's attack, for all its style, was yielding little in the way of results.

Stan Long claimed ignorance on all the major points. He didn't know who killed Hollander, nor what the jester statue meant. "I never cared for Gilbert and Sullivan, I'm afraid."

"When did you first hear about the new will, Mr. Long?"

"Grandfather told us about it at dinner last night. We quarreled with him, of course. Throwing away the family's money on silly entertainment."

It occurred to Klinehart that the money had been *earned* by silly entertainment. But he kept his mouth shut.

"How much would the new will have cost you?"

"He wouldn't say—" Long smiled ruefully. "Oh, was that a trap? I presume the killer saw the will, so he's the only one who knows its exact contents. All grandfather would tell us is that he was decreasing our shares in favor of the opera company. He wouldn't say by how much."

"How are you fixed financially, Mr. Long?"

"I can't complain. In two years' time I'll probably be a vice-president in my corporation." He smiled again. "I don't have to kill for money, Lieutenant."

"When did you go to bed last night?"

"Maureen and I went upstairs as soon as we all returned from the restaurant. Around eleven, I'd say."

"Did you hear anything during the night?"

Long shook his head. "I'm a sound sleeper. It would have taken a *very* loud fight to wake me up. Are we about done here?"

Klinehart noticed the lieutenant took a more direct approach with the next witness, the victim's nephew. "They tell me that you have money problems, Mr. Anson."

"Well, now and then." Douglas Anson was a thin, nervous-looking man of twenty-five. "I'm a free-lance photographer. That means some months are better than others and I admit that I could use a few of the better ones right about now."

"How much would the new will have cost you?"

"I don't know. Uncle Jeremy wouldn't give us any details."

Klinehart saw Perez heave a sigh. "Tell me about the fight in the restaurant."

"Which one?"

The lieutenant looked startled. "How many were there?"

"Two. We quarreled over the will, of course, but before that there was a fight over dinner itself."

"No one mentioned that."

"No one asked us—or at least, no one asked me. The other policeman just wanted to know about the will."

"Well, I'm asking now. What was the quarrel about?"

"Dinner. The restaurant was my cousin Sally's idea, you see. She said it was the best place in town for seafood." Anson grimaced. "She always thinks she knows what's best. We tend to go along with her to keep the peace."

"But not last night?"

"Well, we went to the restaurant she chose, but cousin Stan proceeded to order a steak. It wasn't even on the menu. But they found him one."

Perez frowned. "And that caused a fight?"

"It sure did. Remember, Sally raved all day about the fish and seafood at this joint and then her brother orders steak. She really blew up at him."

Edwards cleared his throat. "Maybe Mr. Long doesn't like fish."

Anson shook his head. "As a matter of fact, he does. He said he just didn't feel like it last night. Sally said he did it just to get her goat, and she was probably right. They don't get along very well."

"How did Mr. Hollander react?"

"I think that, like me, he was amused. We've seen those two go at it before. Then when things began to calm down—meaning that Sally started sulking—Uncle Jeremy dropped the bombshell about his will."

"Who seemed most upset about that, Mr. Anson?"

"We were all pretty irritated, but I suppose Maureen, Stan's wife, was the most insistent that Uncle Jeremy should give us details." He smiled wryly. "Maybe she doesn't know his stubborn streak as well as the rest of us."

"When did you go to bed last night?"

"Right after dinner. I don't know what time it was, but the next thing I heard was Mr. Edwards shouting for help this morning."

"Okay, did you notice—" He stopped because a young woman had appeared in the doorway.

She was very pretty and in fact she reminded Klinehart of the singer who had played the title role in a recent production of *Princess Ida*. He usually fell vaguely in love with the female leads—provided that they sang well, of course.

"I'm very sorry," she said. "I didn't mean to interrupt."

"May I help you, ma'am? I'm Lieutenant Perez."

"I'm Maureen Long. I was looking for my husband, and someone said he was in here."

"He was. I don't know where he is now. As long as you're here, why don't you have a seat and we'll get this done?"

He turned to the photographer. "Thank you, Mr. Anson. I think that's all for now."

Stanley Long's wife was obviously nervous and Klinehart felt sorry for her.

There was something he wanted to say, but before he could phrase it Douglas Anson was out of the room and the interrogation began.

Klinehart sat through the first part in uneasy silence, listening as Ms. Long described the two quarrels at dinner.

"Did you hear anything unusual during the night, Ms. Long?"

"We slept straight through. Stan woke me at eight-thirty when he heard Mr. Edwards shouting downstairs."

"When did you—"

"Excuse me, Lieutenant. May I say something?"

Three surprised faces turned toward Klinehart, who went bright red.

"Yes, Sergeant?"

"I just thought you might want to warn Ms. Long about the penalties for supplying a false alibi."

Everyone was staring and Klinehart wished he was back among his evidence boxes. "You probably think you're safe," he said earnestly, "because you can't be forced to testify against your husband, Ms. Long. But if you *do* testify and lie, that would be perjury. It would also make you an accessory after the fact."

Edwards began to sputter. Perez opened his mouth but before he could speak Maureen Long cut him off in a very effective way: she began to cry.

The next two hours were a blur to Klinehart.

Once it became clear that Maureen Long was accusing her husband of murder, there was a flurry of activity. Lawyers, cops and assistant district attorneys rushed in and out, from one phone to another, from one room to the next, from the mansion to waiting cars and back again.

Even Sally Long made a surprise appearance, unlocking her door for a moment to shriek at the police while they escorted her brother out in handcuffs.

Finally the three men were alone in the library once more. Lieutenant Perez hung up the phone and turned to Klinehart and Edwards.

"Stanley Long just confessed. He claims it was his wife's idea for him to slip down and look at the will. When his grandfather discovered him, he panicked."

Klinehart shook his head loyally. "I can't believe that Ms. Long was involved."

The lieutenant shrugged. "From our point of view all that matters is who was down in the library with a letter opener. We know the answer to that, thanks to you, Sergeant."

Klinehart cleared his throat modestly. "Thank you, sir."

Suddenly Perez was glaring fiercely. "Which brings me to my next point. I hate to quarrel with success, but you should never have pulled a stunt like that. If you suspected Long was the killer, you should have told me."

"I'm very sorry, sir, but I never had the chance. If you remember, Ms. Long came in while you were still questioning Mr. Anson."

Edwards looked up. "You mean it was something Anson said that gave Long away?"

"Yes, sir. This is sort of embarrassing. You see, you and the lieutenant were both right about that statue and I was wrong."

"Spare us the flattery, Sergeant," said Perez. "How did you figure it out?"

"Well, *you* said the statue must be a clue, sir. And Mr. Edwards said that it had to be something simple, like the title of the opera. "

"You're saying *Yeomen of the Guard* indicates Stanley Long?"

"Exactly, sir. It was obvious once Mr. Anson told us about the dinner."

"The dinner? You mean the fact that Long ate steak while the others had fish?"

Klinehart nodded. "Remember, there was quite an argument over it, so the detail was likely to remain in Mr. Hollander's mind. A few hours later, when he needed to identify his grandson as his attacker, that was what he thought of."

"I see the logic, but you still haven't explained how the statue of a jester singled out Stanley Long."

"How?" Klinehart was milking the suspense. He never had such an attentive audience in the evidence room. "I told you the yeomen are the guards at the Tower of London. But they're better known by their nickname."

Edwards winced. "Of course!"

"Of course, what?" said Perez. "What *is* the nickname?"

Klinehart couldn't help grinning. "They're called the Beefeaters, sir."

⚔

Robert Lopresti is the author of more than sixty short stories, which have appeared in *Alfred Hitchcock's Mystery Magazine*, *Ellery Queen's Mystery Magazine*, *The Strand*, and plenty of anthologies. He has won the Derringer and Black Orchid Novella Awards, and been nominated for the Anthony.

THE TERRIBLE TRAGEDY OF LYTTON HOUSE

by David Marcum

FX: A TRAIN STATION, BEFORE THE UPCOMING DEPARTURE OF A TRAIN: CROWD NOISES, CARRIAGE DOORS SLAMMING, WHISTLES

WATSON: *(To himself)* Where can he be? I rushed to the station without stopping for breakfast.

FX: MORE WHISTLES AND SLAMMING DOORS— IMMINENT DEPARTURE

WATSON: *(To himself)* Holmes's note specifically said this train.

HOLMES: *(In the distance, running, out of breath, getting closer)* Watson! What compartment are you in? Watson!

WATSON: *(To himself, relieved)* There he is! *(Louder)* Holmes! Holmes! This way! Hurry man, you'll miss the train!

FX: TRAIN MOVEMENT, SCRAMBLING SOUNDS, DOORS SLAMMING, PEOPLE SETTLING INTO SEATS

HOLMES: *(Out of breath)* Right on time, as usual.

FX: TRAIN NOISES BECOME STEADIER AND MUTED, WITH OCCASIONAL WHISTLES SOFTLY UNDER CONVERSATION

WATSON: Good heavens, Holmes, you nearly missed your footing.

HOLMES: Not at all, Watson. What you perceived as a near
             miss was in fact a carefully calculated effort that
             resulted exactly as I had intended. I anticipated how
             much time I would need to arrive at the station,
             make my way in through the crowds, and to board
             the train without any time wasted. I—

WATSON: Holmes—

HOLMES: I was also aware of what I could expect in terms
             of my own athletic abilities in order to reach and
             board the train at the speed in which it was depart-
             ing.

WATSON: *(Both exasperated and amused)* Norbury.

HOLMES: Hmmm?

WATSON: Norbury, Holmes. *Norbury.* Surely you haven't
             already forgotten? It has only been two weeks
             since the matter of Mr Grant Munro's mysterious
             neighbor. You might recall that you theorized a
             completely incorrect and rather grim solution to Mr
             Munro's problem, and you asked me to—

HOLMES: —I asked you to whisper "Norbury" in my ear—

WATSON: Exactly!

HOLMES: —if I ever again seemed to be becoming over-
             confident in my powers, or not taking the proper
             amount of interest or care in a case. That does not
             apply in this situation.

WATSON: What? Certainly—

HOLMES: In this case, I was not over-confident, I was quite
             accurate in my comprehension of my ability to
             reach the train.

WATSON: Is that why you called out, trying to determine in
             which carriage I was riding?

HOLMES:	What?
WATSON:	You were calling as you ran in order to determine in which carriage I was riding. What would have happened if I had not heard you, or if I was sitting so far forward that you were unable to reach this compartment?
HOLMES:	*(A beat)* I see that we shall have to agree to disagree upon this point.
FX:	RATTLE OF NEWSPAPER BEING RAISED
WATSON:	*(After a short awkward silence)* Well, what were you doing that was so important that you arrived as the train was departing, exactly as you had apparently intended?
FX:	RATTLE OF NEWSPAPER QUICKLY BEING LOWERED
HOLMES:	Research, Watson. This morning I received a wire from Inspector Youghal, requesting our presence in Surrey. Youghal's wire mentioned Lord Bretton, but did not provide any other information, except to state that the matter was urgent. I left a note for you in case you should wish to join me, and then I took a slight detour to ask some questions of that young up-and-coming gossip-monger named Langdale Pike.
WATSON:	Oh-ho, Langdale Pike. Does he still fancy himself as a journalist?
HOLMES:	He is my human book of reference upon all matters relating to society and social scandal.
WATSON:	And what did that strange, languid creature tell you?
HOLMES:	Some basic facts. Lord Bretton has an invalid wife and seven children. The family normally spends

most of the year in London, but they recently returned to their Surrey home, a great run-down place called Lytton House.

WATSON: You risked missing the train and possibly a crippling or fatal injury in order to obtain those facts, which would doubtless have been supplied by Inspector Youghal?

HOLMES: Ah, Watson, I did learn a few other bits which might be of use.

WATSON: And those would be?

HOLMES: That Lord Bretton's finances are in a precarious position, following last year's scandal at the Netherland-Sumatra Company. He has recently been forced to sell his London property to a former business associate, and there are one or two unusual features associated with the sale. His household staff is reduced to a long-time housekeeper from the London house, and a caretaker at the country home. His family is very close-knit and does not mix in society. In fact, his eldest daughter is nineteen years of age and has not been presented. And his wife suffers a debilitating illness, which makes the family's move to Surrey something of a trial.

WATSON: All of that is very informative, but until we find out why Inspector Youghal has summoned us to Surrey, it is meaningless.

HOLMES: That is correct. As you know, I refuse to theorize without data. However, I can consider the facts that we do know in my mind, in case they turn out to be relevant at a later time. And now, Watson, I think I shall smoke a pipe or three and arrange my thoughts. I beg that you do not speak to me for fifty minutes.

MUSIC: SHORT BRIDGE

FX: CARRIAGE SOUNDS (UNDER)

HOLMES: So, Inspector Youghal, please tell us why we are spending this beautiful morning winding our way through the Surrey countryside toward Lytton House?

YOUGHAL: Well, Mr Holmes, it began simple enough. Last Wednesday, Lord Bretton's housekeeper—he only has the one servant down from London right now—noticed that an expensive painting was missing from its usual place in the dining room at the Surrey house. The painting has always been too unwieldy to move back and forth with the family when they live in London, and it is the only thing of real value in the Surrey house—

HOLMES: I'm told that Lord Bretton frequently describes it in private as the most valuable thing that he owns.

YOUGHAL: I've heard something of the sort as well. It may very well be the only thing of value that he owns right now at all, other than the two houses.

WATSON: Actually, Holmes has determined that Lord Bretton recently sold the London house, presumably because he needs the funds.

YOUGHAL: Hmm. In any case, the local police were called in on Wednesday regarding the missing painting, but no obvious clues were discovered. The next day, Thursday, Lord Bretton's youngest child and his only son, Patrick, was last seen at breakfast by the housekeeper, Mrs Jameson, who also serves now as the cook. No one else remembers seeing him for the rest of the day. That evening at dinner, it was finally realized that the boy was missing.

FX: CARRIAGE SOUNDS SLOWING DOWN, HORSE BLOWING WEARILY (UNDER)

YOUGHAL: There it is, gentleman. Lytton House.

WATSON: A picturesque pile, isn't it? It certainly isn't very far from the station. Quite lovely, with all these wide fields and gently flowing hills. But the old farm buildings certainly give it a rather run-down feeling.

HOLMES: Already planning how you'll describe it in your journals, Watson? The fact that a child is missing seems to me to chill the setting, as if one is seeing it while suffering from an illness or fever.

YOUGHAL: That's the truth, Mr Holmes. After the family searched high and low with no success on Thursday night, I was called in yesterday. Once again, we systematically searched the house and grounds, and we have alerted the police in neighboring towns as well. I wasn't getting anywhere, and Lord Bretton, who has heard of you, insisted that you be brought in. Of course, I had no objections, and so this morning I sent you a wire.

HOLMES: *(Sharply)* And today is Saturday, Youghal. We are starting at quite a disadvantage. *(With a more level tone)* Well, it cannot be helped, I suppose.

WATSON: *(Grimly)* A missing child. This is a bad business.

YOUGHAL: I agree, doctor. I always hate a case with a missing child.

FX: CARRIAGE SOUNDS END. MEN CLIMBING DOWN AS THE HORSE SHUFFLES

YOUGHAL: *(Undertone)* This is Lord Bretton, coming toward us now.

FX: FOOTSTEPS APPROACH ACROSS GRAVEL

YOUGHAL: *(Louder)* Lord Bretton, may I introduce Mr Sherlock Holmes and Dr Watson?

BRETTON: Yes, of course. Thank you for coming, Mr Holmes, doctor. I have heard of your successes, and I insisted that Inspector Youghal obtain your assistance in this matter.

HOLMES: *(Impatient)* Yes, quite. May I see the location where the stolen painting hung?

BRETTON: *(Slightly taken aback)* Of course, Mr Holmes. But … but what of my son? Perhaps it would be better—

HOLMES: I have certain questions in my mind that must be answered. To see the path toward finding your son, we must first clear away some of the brush regarding the missing painting, in order to determine if the events are related. If you please?

BRETTON: Certainly, certainly. Follow me to the house. The painting hung in the dining room.

FX: FOOTSTEPS OF SEVERAL MEN ACROSS A WOODEN FLOOR, DOOR OPENING

BRETTON: In here, Mr Holmes. You can see that large, rather faded patch on the wall, where the painting has hung for more years than I can tell.

FX: MENS' FOOTSTEPS END. MORE FOOTSTEPS FADE IN (LIGHTER, A WOMAN)

BRETTON: Ah, my dear. Gentlemen, may I introduce my oldest daughter, Emily. She is quite the lady of the house, due to my wife's unfortunate illness.

(Ad-lib general greetings: Nice to meet you, etc.)

EMILY: Thank you for coming, gentlemen. We're most grateful.

BRETTON: Mr Holmes wants to know about the missing painting, my dear.

EMILY: The painting? But surely … surely that is not why you are here. I thought that father summoned you regarding my brother, Patrick.

HOLMES: As I explained to your father, miss, I must determine what the relationship is, if any, between the two incidents. What can you tell me about the painting?

EMILY: *(Confused)* Of course. Well, it is a rather obscure Constable. A landscape of the local area, I believe. Although it is not one of his better known works, it is considered to be somewhat valuable. It is quite large, and covered most of that wall, as you can see. The frame is rather solid, and is itself considered on its own to be something of a work of art—

HOLMES: Perhaps I should have been more specific. Do you have any facts which might throw light on how the painting came to disappear?

EMILY: Why, no, Mr Holmes. The painting was discovered to be missing on Wednesday morning by Mrs Jameson. *(With more emotion)* Why are you wasting time looking for the painting? It had already been found missing and investigated by the police a full day before Patrick vanished.

BRETTON: Now, now, Emily, Mr Holmes knows his business. Dry your eyes, and run along and check on your sisters.

EMILY: Yes, father. *(Sniffs)* It was good to meet you, gentlemen.

FX: WOMAN'S FOOTSTEPS FADING

BRETTON: Poor girl. This has affected her terribly. I don't know what I would do without her. Since my poor wife has been ill, and since my unfortunate … financial reversals last year, it has been necessary for Emily to assume a great many additional responsibilities around the house. And she is like a second mother to the children. I assure you, gentlemen, that a house filled with six daughters and a young son .... *(Stops, chokes with emotion)*

FX: BOOT FOOTSTEPS QUICKLY ON WOODEN FLOOR

HOLMES: *(Briskly)* This window has been recently opened.

BRETTON: *(Composing himself)* Impossible, Mr Holmes. We keep that window shut, even in summertime. The prevailing winds on this side of the house tend to cause terrible drafts in here. The drapes become tangled, the candles gutter terribly, and of course we want to protect the painting from the elements.

FX: SOUND OF WINDOW OPENING

HOLMES: *(Softly, to himself)* The ground outside is gravel. No footprints. But what is this on the window-sill? *(Louder)* Nevertheless, this window has been opened, and recently. How often does this room get used?

FX: SOUND OF WINDOW CLOSING

BRETTON: Rarely, Mr Holmes. Our family tends to eat in the smaller, less formal room, toward the rear of the house. The last time that we ate in here was a week ago, last Saturday, when we had a guest down from London.

HOLMES: A guest? And who might that have been, Lord Bretton?

BRETTON: Why, my former business partner, Sir Sheffield Frye. He is an old friend of mine and a frequent visitor at our London home, but this was the first time that he had joined us here in the wilds of Surrey. We had a bit of business to transact, and he accepted my invitation to visit and dine here. Sir Sheffield is a great favorite of all of us.

HOLMES: I see. And when did Sir Sheffield return to London?

BRETTON: On Sunday morning. I took him in the dogcart to the station myself. *(Quieter)* There was some difficulty at the time, you see. The caretaker was … unavailable, and I didn't mind driving, since we—since we no longer have a coachman.

HOLMES: Quite. And now, I believe I would like to question the staff.

BRETTON: Certainly. I'll send in Mrs Jameson, the housekeeper, and then the caretaker. I have a list of instructions to pass along to Emily as well. Dr Watson, I wonder—as long as you're here—if you wouldn't mind checking on my wife …

WATSON: Certainly. Lead the way, Lord Bretton.

FX: MEN'S FOOTSTEPS ON WOODEN FLOOR FADING

YOUGHAL: *(Softly)* That poor sad girl. Did you see the tears in her eyes? *(Louder)* What did you see at the window, Mr Holmes?

HOLMES: *(Softly, almost to himself)* The sill has been rubbed, as if something—the painting, no doubt—was passed through. There are no marks upon the ground.

YOUGHAL: Do you see any light yet about the boy? Anything at all?

HOLMES: *(Louder)* Data, Youghal, data! I must have clay to make bricks!

MUSIC: SHORT BRIDGE

WATSON: Lady Bretton will be unable to tell us anything. Between her illness and her worry, she is just one short step away from brain fever.

YOUGHAL: Well, Mrs Jameson certainly had nothing to add, either. She's more like a member of the family than a housekeeper. That one poor woman serves the needs of the entire family, dividing her time between the invalid lady of the house, the children, and the cooking duties as well.

HOLMES: We did learn a few relevant facts. Mrs Jameson believes that the sale of the London house was somewhat sudden, and also understands that there will not be an increase of staff at this house, reflecting Lord Bretton's continued financial difficulties.

YOUGHAL: Also, she said that most of this building will continue to remain closed on a permanent basis, with only a few rooms reopened for use by the family, as it has been on those past occasions when they previously journeyed here from London in the spring and summer months. We searched the entire building yesterday, from top to bottom. There was no sign of Patrick, or the missing painting in any of those closed rooms. I'll swear to that.

HOLMES: Then far be it from me to have it searched again, Youghal.

FX: DOOR OPENS, MAN'S FOOTSTEPS APPROACH

HOLMES: Ah, you must be Jonas, the caretaker. We were just discussing yesterday's search of the house. What can you tell me about the search of the grounds?

FX: FOOTSTEPS END, CHAIR SCRAPING

JONAS: *(Somewhat surly)* Well, they were searched very well, indeed. We went over the whole estate, including all of the old outbuildings and that small woodland to the south side. Took me away from my regular duties—

YOUGHAL: Here now, what regular duties might you have that are more important that searching for the master's missing son?

JONAS: *(Whining)* I'm the only man here, and I'm expected to take care of the whole place, and to keep things presentable without any assistance at all. And now the housekeeper tells me that the family has sold their London home and will be living here year round. Yet there has been no mention of getting any help for poor old Jonas, now has there?

WATSON: *(Trying to calm things down)* Jonas, we're simply trying to find out if you can provide any information that will help us locate young Patrick.

JONAS: I did what I could. I helped in the search. We looked everywhere, some places more than once. There was even some talk of dragging the mere ....

HOLMES: Yes, yes. Hopefully it won't come to that. Jonas, what can you tell us of Lord Bretton's family?

JONAS: Oh, no objections, I suppose.

YOUGHAL: What? You don't object to them!

JONAS: *(Snapping)* Well, I don't know a thing.

YOUGHAL: Watch your tongue, man!

JONAS: I've nothing to tell you, *sir*. They're a quiet family. They keep to themselves. When they *are* down from London, they all stay inside, all except Miss Emily.

WATSON: What do you mean?

JONAS: Miss Emily is the only one who ever really gets outside and walks over the grounds at any length and explores them. Between you and me, I think she wants some time to herself. She probably knows the place better than I do. It's been that way ever since Lord Bretton bought the place.

YOUGHAL: Bought the place? I thought this was his Lordship's family estate.

JONAS: Oh, no. No, *sir*. The previous owners all died out a few years ago and Lord Bretton bought it at a bargain soon after. I hadn't been here for very long myself then, and Lord Bretton kept me around as caretaker when he let the rest of the staff go.

WATSON: How often do you see young Patrick? It strikes me that a young boy would want to get outside as often as possible.

JONAS: Well, he tries. I think that he would go out more, if his mother would allow it, but he's kept in as much as possible. *(Lowering his voice)* Can I tell you gentlemen what I think?

YOUGHAL: Certainly, certainly.

JONAS: It seems to me that if the family didn't have to live here, because of Lord Bretton's financial misfortunes, they wouldn't.

HOLMES: What do you know of the family finances?

JONAS: *(Softly)* Mrs Jameson told me that the master's funds are limited, and getting worse. Nearly gone, as a matter of fact. That probably explains why he hasn't made any improvements here since he's owned the place. Some parts of the house are in desperate need of repairs, and some of the outbuildings and old barns are near falling down. Mrs Jameson even said that he may be forced to sell this place soon, as well.

HOLMES: And what can you tell us of the missing painting?

JONAS: I've seen it, of course, when I've checked on the house while the family was in London.

WATSON: Do you have any idea where the painting might be, or how it was taken? We understand that it is rather large and cumbersome.

JONAS: No, I don't, and anybody that says different will answer to me. But I can tell you that it wouldn't be an easy thing to move, what with how big it is, and how it's in that great heavy frame.

HOLMES: Hmm .... How often does the family have visitors here at the Surrey home?

JONAS: Never, Mr Holmes. I've heard from Mrs Jameson that it's the same at the London house. They're a very close bunch, they are.

WATSON: Jonas, you said the family does not have visitors, yet we have been told that Sir Sheffield Frye was down just a week ago today.

JONAS: Oh, well, that is right. I forgot about him. He was just here for the one night. This was his first trip down to this house.

HOLMES: Why didn't you drive Sir Sheffield to the station last Sunday morning when it was time for his departure? Why was Lord Bretton forced to drive him in the dogcart?

JONAS: *(Suddenly hostile)* And why do you need to know about that? That doesn't have anything to do with anything!

YOUGHAL: Answer the question!

JONAS: Well, I ... I suppose that I was unavailable then. I must have been out taking care of something on the estate.

YOUGHAL: *(Sarcastically)* Of course you were, early on a Sunday morning. *(More stern)* Jonas, do you have any knowledge concerning young Patrick's whereabouts?

JONAS: No. No, sir, but I can hardly blame the young scamp for running away.

WATSON: So you believe that he ran away, then?

JONAS: Well, it stands to reason, don't it? The only boy with six older sisters? That would have been enough to make me run away when I was a lad. I remember the time when the circus came to our village. There was this lady bareback rider. I thought that she—

WATSON: Really? I also—

HOLMES: *(Hastily)* Quite, quite. Thank you for your assistance, Jonas, and we'll let you know if we have any further questions.

FX: CHAIR SCRAPING, FOOTSTEPS (FADING), DOOR CLOSING

WATSON: That certainly didn't add anything useful.

YOUGHAL: Well, I don't trust him. A man like that, having the run of an estate such as this for most of the year, suddenly finding out that he's going to be expected to work a full day again year round?

WATSON: And then he avoids the duties that he does have. From what I could judge of the man's appearance and character, I'm sure that he was unable to drive Sir Sheffield Frye to the station last Sunday morning because he was recovering from a trip to the local pub on Saturday night. Do you agree, Holmes? Did you learn anything from the conversation?

HOLMES:	*(Distracted)* What? Oh, certainly, Watson. He exhibited all the signs of a chronic drunkard. And yet, if I'm not mistaken, he's hiding something—
FX:	DOOR OPENS; MAN'S FOOTSTEPS ENTER AND STOP
HOLMES:	Ah, Lord Bretton. Just the man I wanted to see. I have another question for you.
BRETTON:	Yes, Mr Holmes?
HOLMES:	We have been given to understand that you have sold your London home. Is that correct?
BRETTON:	*(Quiet, embarrassed)* Yes, that is true, Mr Holmes. To my friend Sir Sheffield Frye. That was why he came down last Saturday, to deliver the proof of payment and the final copy of the papers.
HOLMES:	May I see those documents, Lord Bretton?
BRETTON:	Certainly. Although I don't see how— That is, I'll have them for you momentarily.
FX:	FOOTSTEPS (FADING)
WATSON:	*(Softly)* Holmes, what do you make of this business? Do you see any hope?
HOLMES:	*(Softly)* These are dark waters, Watson. I have a dim perception of what may have happened, but I hope I am wrong. Let us both hope that I am wrong!
MUSIC:	SHORT BRIDGE
FX:	MENS FOOTSTEPS ON GRASS, BIRDS SINGING
WATSON:	Did you learn anything from the documents, Holmes?
HOLMES:	Hmmm … they confirmed some of what Langdale Pike related to me this morning. Unfortunately, I

believe that a conversation with Sir Sheffield in person in London is now unavoidable.

YOUGHAL: Mr Holmes, I fail to see how traveling to London to interview Sir Sheffield Frye will get us any closer to finding the missing boy. If it was a question of ransom— But no ransom note has been received.

HOLMES: Nevertheless, everything indicates to me that we need to understand all that has happened here, starting a week ago, in order to get at the entire truth. We must run up to London immediately, and attempt to corner Sir Sheffield Frye.

MUSIC: SHORT BRIDGE

FX: CAROUSING NOISES (GLASSES CLINKING, RANDOM CONVERSATION) UNDER

WATSON: *(Softly)* There he is, Holmes. Over there, at the card table.

YOUGHAL: We've only had to track him across half of London before finding him here at the Nonpareil Club.

HOLMES: He appears to be somewhat inebriated. That may work to our advantage.

YOUGHAL: How, Mr Holmes? I must admit that your theory, whatever it is, certainly seems to be correct. We found the painting, right where you said it would be. But I cannot see a connection between Sir Sheffield and the missing boy. And we cannot just walk up to a peer and imply that there is one.

HOLMES: *You* cannot, inspector. As you are now aware, Sir Sheffield is tied to the missing painting. And it appears more and more likely that the painting is related to the missing boy. *(Louder)* Sir Sheffield Frye? Perhaps you remember when we met last year, during the events of the Netherland-Sumatra affair? This is Dr Watson, and Inspector Youghal of Scotland Yard. My name is—

FRYE: *(Somewhat intoxicated)* Of course I remember you. Mr Sherlock Holmes. Holmes, the meddler. Well, what do you want? The cards are hot, man. Don't you understand what that means?

HOLMES: This may only take a few moments, Sir Sheffield, depending on your response. If we could just step over here, into this side room?

FX: CHAIR SCRAPING, FOOTSTEPS. CAROUSING NOISES BECOMING MORE MUTED UNTIL DOOR CLOSES

FRYE: *(Impatient)* What is it, Holmes?

HOLMES: We simply need for you to tell us, Sir Sheffield, what were the specific arrangements for stealing Lord Bretton's painting from the Surrey house?

YOUGHAL: *(Shocked, surprised)* Mr Holmes? A moment ...?

WATSON: *(Softly)* Trust him, Youghal.

YOUGHAL: Mr Holmes, you can't just—

FRYE: *(Sputters)* Steal his— Steal his painting? I have stolen *nothing*!

HOLMES: Sir Sheffield? Our time is precious, and your prevarication is wasted. The details, if you please.

FRYE: Inspector, I sense that you are not a willing participant in this slanderous behavior, but I assure you that your superiors will be made aware of this incident.

YOUGHAL: *(Urgent, quiet)* Mr Holmes, could we converse outside?

HOLMES: *(Ignoring Youghal. Quiet, cold, completely in control)* Sir Sheffield, you will tell me the details of how you took possession of the painting, for I need to determine if my conclusions regarding its connection with Lord Bretton's missing son are correct. Only by clearing up the mystery surrounding the painting can we see about locating the boy.

YOUGHAL: *(Softly)* Doctor, do you know what Mr Holmes is about?

WATSON: *(Softly)* I begin to have a dim perception. I hope that I'm wrong.

FRYE: *(More sober)* Bretton's son is missing? What has that to do with me? He was just fine when I ... when I last saw him.

HOLMES: And when was that?

FRYE: Why, last Saturday, a week ago, of course. When I was at their Surrey home for dinner.

HOLMES: And if I tell you that you were seen when you returned to Surrey a few days later?

FRYE: Impossible! No one saw me—

HOLMES: Are you certain of that?

FRYE: *(Still a little drunk)* Why, I ... I ... No one saw me. You're bluffing!

WATSON: *(Quietly)* Holmes, it's almost unfair to take advantage of the man in his intoxicated state.

HOLMES: I have read the document that you prepared in order to purchase Lord Bretton's London house, Sir Sheffield. The odd clause that it contains helped me to understand what you intended.

YOUGHAL: Odd clause? I didn't notice anything unusual.

WATSON: I'm sure that we saw it, Youghal, but we did not observe it. It is a rather familiar experience for me.

HOLMES: The clause states that you were not only buying the London house, but whatever contents were contained within it at the time of purchase, without question. Those were the papers that you delivered when you visited the Surrey home last Saturday, one week ago today. Is that correct?

FRYE: Yes, yes. Of course. But that has nothing to do with the painting.

HOLMES: That isn't true, Sir Sheffield. You specifically included that particular and rather unusual clause so that you could claim ownership of the Constable painting, which had been accurately and repeatedly described to you by Lord Bretton as the most valuable thing that he owned. You intended to carry the painting back to London with you in secret when you left Surrey on Sunday morning, did you not, so it would be in the London house when the sale was finalized on Monday, thus making it your property?

YOUGHAL: Of course! As they say, possession is nine-tenths of the law.

WATSON: A fine way to treat your friend.

FRYE: *(Snarls)* Friend? What kind of a friend was he last year, during the Netherland-Sumatra affair? His idiocy nearly cost me everything that I had. He was too afraid to take the risks that were needed in order to save himself, and he nearly brought me down as well. I've had to work like the devil over the last year to recoup my losses. And then the fool comes to me and asks me to help him out of a hole for old time's sake by buying his London home, so that he'll have a little cash to live on for a while longer in Surrey.

HOLMES: That is *your* perception of the events of last year. You forget that I have some knowledge of the matter, as well. There is every indication that Lord Bretton's financial disaster was due to *you*, Sir Sheffield, and his foolish trust in *your* advice. Nevertheless, I'm certain that you have convinced yourself of your own innocence in the matter, and that you also convinced your accomplice in order to gain assistance in taking the painting.

YOUGHAL: Accomplice?

HOLMES: Of course. There had to be someone in the house who could inform Sir Sheffield that the painting would not immediately be missed. This person was also required to help make the arrangements with Jonas, in order to transport the painting to the train station on Sunday morning.

FRYE: *(To himself)* That drunken fool ….

HOLMES: No doubt the plan was for Sir Sheffield to leave with the painting early on Sunday, catching the milk train before the family was even awake. By the time Sir Sheffield and his co-conspirator realized that they would not have Jonas's help due to his inebriated state, and that it was too late to remove the painting that morning, Lord Bretton was up. Alternate plans were quickly made, and Sir Sheffield was forced to return later in the week to collect the painting.

FRYE: You devil! You don't know what you're talking about!

WATSON: We've seen the painting, Sir Sheffield. We've been to Lord Bretton's former London home, where it is hanging in the dining room as if it had always been there.

YOUGHAL: But Mr Holmes, the family would have realized who took it, and how Sir Sheffield had swindled them with the wording of the contract. They would have been able to tell the authorities what had happened.

HOLMES: Not *all* of the family, Youghal.

WATSON: Of course. The accomplice would have lied for Sir Sheffield.

HOLMES: Very good, Watson. I see that you've caught up.

WATSON: It would have been their word against the rest of the family. What did you promise her, Sir Sheffield? Marriage?

FRYE: *(Grudgingly)* We had an arrangement. She said that she loved me. I ... I suppose that I have feelings for her as well. She was going to leave her family to be with me.

YOUGHAL: She? It can't be the housekeeper? She was the one that reported the painting as being missing. And Lady Bretton is an invalid. Then the accomplice must be—

WATSON: Congratulations, inspector. Now you are caught up as well.

HOLMES: *(Ignoring them)* According to my watch—

FX: POCKET WATCH SNAPS OPEN

HOLMES: —we have unfortunately missed the last train back to Surrey.

FX: POCKET WATCH SNAPS SHUT

HOLMES: However, Sir Sheffield, I am afraid that your card game is over. Inspector, have one of your men take him into custody. I must send a lengthy wire with instructions to the Surrey constabulary, and then Sir Sheffield will provide us with additional information while we arrange for transportation back to Lytton House.

MUSIC: SHORT BRIDGE

FX: FOOTSTEPS THROUGH GRASS

HOLMES: (*Angry*) Blast the trains! It would have been faster to have hired a carriage!

WATSON: We did what we could. We wired the local police. They were able to—

YOUGHAL: (*Out of breath, joining them*) The family is waiting at the house. I haven't told them anything. They all remained indoors while we were gone, much as we left them. After you sent your wire, Mr Holmes, my men searched and found several abandoned barns and outbuildings on the south edge of the property. It took them a while to identify the right one, and to search it in order to find what they were looking for.

WATSON: And was it as we feared?

FX: FOOTSTEPS THROUGH GRASS OUT

YOUGHAL: (*A pause, and then quietly somber*) I'm told that we'd better see for ourselves ....

FX: BARN DOOR CREAKS OPEN, FOOTSTEPS ACROSS HOLLOW-SOUNDING BOARDS

YOUGHAL: (*Muffled from being inside the dusty barn*) Over here, gentlemen. My men said it was in the middle of the floor. Careful, watch your step ... Down there.

WATSON: (*Softly*) Oh, my God.

HOLMES: (*Pause, then quietly*) Let us go back to the house.

MUSIC: SHORT BRIDGE

FX: MAIN DOOR OPENING, MENS' FOOTSTEPS ENTER AND STOP

HOLMES: Where are they, Youghal?

YOUGHAL: Lord Bretton and Emily are in the dining room. The other children and Lady Bretton are upstairs.

WATSON: Well, let's get this over with.

FX: DOOR OPENING, MEN'S FOOTSTEPS ENTER, STOP

HOLMES: *(Deep breath)* Lord Bretton, I am afraid that I have some terrible news.

BRETTON: *(With dread)* Patrick?

HOLMES: *(Very quiet)* I am sorry, sir. Your son is dead.

BRETTON: *(Anguished)* No! *(Softer)* No ….

EMILY: What? How— What has happened, Mr Holmes?

BRETTON: *(Softly, gaining control of himself)* Yes, please, what has happened?

HOLMES: Last night, Inspector Youghal, Dr Watson, and I located Sir Sheffield Frye in London—

BRETTON: *(Less emotional, puzzled)* Sir Sheffield Frye?

HOLMES: Yes, Lord Bretton. He has poorly repaid your trust in him as a guest. After we found Sir Sheffield at his club, it was a quick matter to get the complete story out of him. During his visits to your London home, he had been secretly romancing Emily. *(Tone changes, more harsh)* Not necessarily because he cared anything about her, of course. He was simply dallying with her, as he has with others before her, always on the lookout for an opportunity if one should present itself.

EMILY: *(Simply a statement of fact)* He loves me.

FX: MAN'S FOOTSTEPS AS YOUGHAL STEPS BEHIND EMILY

BRETTON: Inspector, why are you gripping my daughter's shoulder?

WATSON: When you asked him to buy the London property, in order to save you financially, his initial response was to turn you down. He blames you for his reversals last year. However, it occurred to him that he could maneuver events so that he could gain ownership of the Constable painting. He could then sell it for more than he was paying you for the house, thus turning a profit, and still have the London house as well. He managed to get Emily to help him, believing that he could keep her quiet with further empty promises of love, and that the painting's theft wouldn't immediately be discovered. Later, with Emily under his thumb and backing up his version of events, the threat of scandal might silence the family if necessary.

BRETTON: I don't believe it. Emily ....

HOLMES: Emily removed the painting from the house and hid it in a root cellar in of the abandoned barns on the property. Unexpectedly, the painting was discovered missing on Wednesday. Emily, who volunteered to go to town to summon the police, also sent word to Sir Sheffield to stay away until the next day, Thursday, without telling him why. On Thursday morning she slipped away, intending to meet Frye at the barn and give him the painting.

BRETTON: *(Horrified)* Emily. Tell them it isn't true, Emily ....

WATSON: We learned this much from Sir Sheffield last night. He showed up on Thursday to receive the painting as planned. Of course, it had not been discovered the previous day by the police during their searches. They had paid scant attention to the abandoned building, and they hadn't even realized that there was a root cellar.

HOLMES: Sir Sheffield met Emily at the shed as arranged. As Frye took possession of the canvas, he was dismayed to hear Patrick, watching them through a crack in the building's wall.

MUSIC: SHORT BRIDGE

FRYE: *(Irritated)* What took you so long, girl? What if someone sees me or my wagon?

EMILY: *(Snappish, not like the Emily we've previously met at all)* I got here as quickly as I could. Jonas won't see you. He's drunk as usual, and asleep in his cottage. Everyone else is inside. They never come out, and we're well away from the house out here. Besides, I had to make sure that the police hadn't come back.

FRYE: *(Urgent)* The police? Do you mean to say they have already discovered that the painting is gone? You said the dining room where it hung goes unused for weeks!

EMILY: I thought that no one would notice that it was gone, but yesterday, the housekeeper saw that it was missing. Father insisted on calling in the police. It's the only thing of value that he still owns. I don't have to tell you how he's thrown everything else away. After you and I are married, perhaps we'll give him a little money. Maybe we'll make him beg for it. It will be nice to have him beholden to me for a change.

FRYE: Where is the root cellar?

EMILY: Over here. Help me ….

FX: FOOTSTEPS ACROSS HOLLOW SOUNDING BOARDS. TRAP DOOR RAISING

EMILY: No, you don't have to climb down. It's not deep. Just reach in. I've turned the frame up on its side. It almost reaches the top of the cellar. Turn it, more, sideways, that's it ….

FX:	SCRAMBLING SOUNDS, HEAVY BREATHING
FRYE:	Got it! Now—*(grunting)*—let's get it in the wag-on—
FX:	PAINTING BEING LIFTED OUT AND LOADED INTO THE WAGON
FRYE:	There!
FX:	SOME LOGS SHIFT, MAKING A NOISE
FRYE:	What's that! Oh, dear lord, it's your brother!
EMILY:	*(Urgent)* Run, Sheff! Run! I'll take care of Patrick!
FRYE:	But—
EMILY:	Run!
FX:	RUNNING FOOTSTEPS CLIMBING INTO THE WAGON, HORSE AND WAGON DEPARTURE (FADING)
EMILY:	*(Softly, to herself)* I'll be with you soon, my love.
MUSIC:	SHORT BRIDGE
HOLMES:	*(Softly)* We went out to the abandoned barn a few moments ago. The trapdoor to the root cellar had been closed, and covered by straw so that it would not be found, except by someone who already knew that it was there. Were you aware that there was a root cellar in that building, Lord Bretton?
BRETTON:	*(Whispers)* No. *(Clears his throat)* No, I had no idea.
HOLMES:	We just spoke to Jonas, and he was unaware of it, as well. It is not much of a chamber, a mere five feet or so deep, and about the same area square. It is likely that unless you had plans to remove the building anytime soon, the whole thing would have continued its slow collapse on top of the chamber,

and no one would have realized for many years, if ever, that it was there.

(Quietly) When we looked inside, we were dismayed to find the body of young Patrick.

BRETTON: *(Sobbing sound, softly)* Oh! Oh, my son!

WATSON: *(Softly)* Holmes ....

HOLMES: The boy had been wounded gravely on the head. A piece of bloodstained wood, cut for stove length, was tossed down beside the body.

YOUGHAL: *(Roughly, his voice cracking with emotion)* She had thrown lime over the boy. She didn't want him to be found. She covered up the trap door.

EMILY: *(Matter-of-fact)* Inspector, you are hurting my arm.

HOLMES: Sir Sheffield said that Emily believed that he was going to marry her. Of course, he never had any intention of that, since he is already married.

EMILY: *(Surprised)* What? You lie!

HOLMES: *(With an edge)* No doubt she feared if her perfidy were discovered too soon, her plans to be with Sir Sheffield would fall through. Perhaps she did not mean to kill Patrick, and only lashed out unthinkingly to stop him. However, once the deed was done, she deliberately hid the body, fixing it so that it would not be found. She threw lime liberally into the hole, in order to minimize the problems associated with decomposition. There was no lime stored in the abandoned building, so she would have had to get it from elsewhere on the grounds. This took intentional effort and planning. Then she covered the trap door with straw to make certain that the boy would not be found during the subsequent search which was sure to be made over the entire estate.

EMILY:	*(Confused, and somewhat irritated, to herself)* Why did Sheff tell? No one would have ever known. He could have sold the painting, and then he would have come for me. Then I wouldn't have had to take care of the children any more. *(Softer)* I've never liked children.
BRETTON:	*(In horror)* Emily—
YOUGHAL:	*(Clearing his throat)* Constable. Constable!
FX:	MUFFLED FOOTSTEPS, DOOR OPENING, LOUDER FOOSTEPS
YOUGHAL:	Take her in charge. And make sure that no one goes upstairs and tells the mother or children what's happened yet. The lady is in poor health, and I want to make sure she that she finds this out as mercifully as possible.
MUSIC:	SHORT BRIDGE
FX:	OUTSIDE: BIRDS SINGING. FOOTSTEPS ON GRAVEL AND UNDER
YOUGHAL:	Doctor, how is Lady Bretton?
WATSON:	Not well, inspector. Not well.
YOUGHAL:	*(Clears his throat)* Can I offer you gentlemen a ride back to the station? The carriage is waiting right over here.
WATSON:	The one containing Emily and the constable? I don't fancy making the trip while staring at the mad, reddish wet gaze of that deluded young woman.
HOLMES:	*(Quietly)* Very descriptive, Watson. *(Louder)* Thank you, Youghal, but I believe that we shall find our own way back to town.
MUSIC:	SHORT BRIDGE

HOLMES: I believe that they will find her to be quite mad. I am afraid Lord Bretton's family is only at the beginning of their pain. Their only son and brother dead, and they have to live for years with the constant reminder of what happened in the form of Emily, who will no doubt be hospitalized for quite a long time. I do not see her condition improving.

WATSON: And Sir Sheffield Frye?

HOLMES: He will get a few years for the attempted theft of the painting, but he was clearly not involved in the murder. I hope that this will serve to break him, but a rogue like that will no doubt rise from all of this like some sort of phoenix.

FX: HOLMES REACHES FOR THE VIOLIN, PLUCKING AND TUNING THE STRINGS. HE STOPS

HOLMES: Do you know, Watson, Lord Bretton described that painting as his most valuable possession. How sad for him to realize only now that his most valuable possessions are his children.

FX: HOLMES DRAGS THE BOW ACROSS THE STRINGS

HOLMES: Do you mind if I play for a while? Will it disturb you?

WATSON: No, Holmes. *(Pause)* Please play. *(Pause)* Good night.

HOLMES: Good night, Watson.

MUSIC: Mournful Notes, fading away ....

David Marcum is the author of *The Papers of Sherlock Holmes, Volumes I & II* and *Sherlock Holmes and A Quantity of Debt*, available from MX Publishing.

This play was first performed by Imagination Theater, and broadcast nationwide on November 24, 2013. John Patrick Lowrie played Sherlock Holmes, and Lawrence Albert was Dr Watson.

THE ADVENTURE OF THE ENGINEER'S THUMB

by Sir Arthur Conan Doyle

Of all the problems which have been submitted to my friend, Mr. Sherlock Holmes, for solution during the years of our intimacy, there were only two which I was the means of introducing to his notice—that of Mr. Hatherley's thumb, and that of Colonel Warburton's madness. Of these the latter may have afforded a finer field for an acute and original observer, but the other was so strange in its inception and so dramatic in its details that it may be the more worthy of being placed upon record, even if it gave my friend fewer openings for those deductive methods of reasoning by which he achieved such remarkable results. The story has, I believe, been told more than once in the newspapers, but, like all such narratives, its effect is much less striking when set forth *en bloc* in a single half-column of print than when the facts slowly evolve before your own eyes, and the mystery clears gradually away as each new discovery furnishes a step which leads on to the complete truth. At the time the circumstances made a deep impression upon me, and the lapse of two years has hardly served to weaken the effect.

It was in the summer of '89, not long after my marriage, that the events occurred which I am now about to summarize. I had returned to civil practice and had finally abandoned Holmes in his Baker Street rooms, although I continually visited him and occasionally even persuaded him to forgo his Bohemian habits so far as to come and visit us. My practice had steadily increased, and as I happened to live at no very great distance from Paddington Station, I got a few patients from among the officials. One of these, whom I had cured of a painful and lingering disease, was never weary of advertising my virtues and of endeavoring to send me on every sufferer over whom he might have any influence.

One morning, at a little before seven o'clock, I was awakened by the maid tapping at the door to announce that two men had come from Paddington and were waiting in the consulting-room. I dressed hurriedly, for I knew by experience that railway cases were seldom trivial, and hastened downstairs. As I descended, my old ally, the guard, came out of the room and closed the door tightly behind him.

"I've got him here," he whispered, jerking his thumb over his shoulder; "he's all right."

"What is it, then?" I asked, for his manner suggested that it was some strange creature which he had caged up in my room.

"It's a new patient," he whispered. "I thought I'd bring him round myself; then he couldn't slip away. There he is, all safe and sound. I must go now, Doctor; I have my dooties, just the same as you." And off he went, this trusty tout, without even giving me time to thank him.

I entered my consulting-room and found a gentleman seated by the table. He was quietly dressed in a suit of heather tweed with a soft cloth cap which he had laid down upon my books. Round one of his hands he had a handkerchief wrapped, which was mottled all over with bloodstains. He was young, not more than five-and-twenty, I should say, with a strong, masculine face; but he was exceedingly pale and gave me the impression of a man who was suffering from some strong agitation, which it took all his strength of mind to control.

"I am sorry to knock you up so early, Doctor," said he, "but I have had a very serious accident during the night. I came in by train this morning, and on inquiring at Paddington as to where I might find a doctor, a worthy fellow very kindly escorted me here. I gave the maid a card, but I see that she has left it upon the side-table."

I took it up and glanced at it. "Mr. Victor Hatherley, hydraulic engineer, 16A, Victoria Street (3rd floor)." That was the name, style, and abode of my morning visitor. "I regret that I have kept you waiting," said I, sitting down in my library-chair. "You are fresh from a night journey, I understand, which is in itself a monotonous occupation."

"Oh, my night could not be called monotonous," said he, and laughed. He laughed very heartily, with a high, ringing note, leaning back in his chair and shaking his sides. All my medical instincts rose up against that laugh.

"Stop it!" I cried; "pull yourself together!" and I poured out some water from a carafe. It was useless, however. He was off in one of those hysterical outbursts which come upon a strong nature when some great crisis is over and gone. Presently he came to himself once more, very weary and pale-looking.

"I have been making a fool of myself," he gasped.

"Not at all. Drink this." I dashed some brandy into the water, and the colour began to come back to his bloodless cheeks.

"That's better!" said he. "And now, Doctor, perhaps you would kindly attend to my thumb, or rather to the place where my thumb used to be."

He unwound the handkerchief and held out his hand. It gave even my hardened nerves a shudder to look at it. There were four protruding fingers and a horrid red, spongy surface where the thumb should have been. It had been hacked or torn right out from the roots.

"Good heavens!" I cried, "this is a terrible injury. It must have bled considerably."

"Yes, it did. I fainted when it was done, and I think that I must have been senseless for a long time. When I came to I found that it was still bleeding, so I tied one end of my handkerchief very tightly round the wrist and braced it up with a twig."

"Excellent! You should have been a surgeon."

"It is a question of hydraulics, you see, and came within my own province."

"This has been done," said I, examining the wound, "by a very heavy and sharp instrument."

"A thing like a cleaver," said he.

"An accident, I presume?"

"By no means."

"What! a murderous attack?"

"Very murderous, indeed."

"You horrify me."

I sponged the wound, cleaned it, dressed it, and finally covered it over with cotton wadding and carbolized bandages. He lay back without wincing, though he bit his lip from time to time.

"How is that?" I asked when I had finished.

"Capital! Between your brandy and your bandage, I feel a new man. I was very weak, but I have had a good deal to go through."

"Perhaps you had better not speak of the matter. It is evidently trying to your nerves."

"Oh, no, not now. I shall have to tell my tale to the police; but, between ourselves, if it were not for the convincing evidence of this wound of mine, I should be surprised if they believed my statement, for it is a very extraordinary one, and I have not much in the way of proof with which to back it up; and, even if they believe me, the clues which I can give them are so vague that it is a question whether justice will be done."

"Ha!" cried I, "if it is anything in the nature of a problem which you desire to see solved, I should strongly recommend you to come to my friend, Mr Sherlock Holmes, before you go to the official police."

"Oh, I have heard of that fellow," answered my visitor, "and I should be very glad if he would take the matter up, though of course I must use the official police as well. Would you give me an introduction to him?"

"I'll do better. I'll take you round to him myself."

"I should be immensely obliged to you."

"We'll call a cab and go together. We shall just be in time to have a little breakfast with him. Do you feel equal to it?"

"Yes; I shall not feel easy until I have told my story."

"Then my servant will call a cab, and I shall be with you in an instant." I rushed upstairs, explained the matter shortly to my wife, and in five minutes was inside a hansom, driving with my new acquaintance to Baker Street.

Sherlock Holmes was, as I expected, lounging about his sitting-room in his dressing-gown, reading the agony column of *The Times* and smoking his before-breakfast pipe, which was composed of all the plugs and dottles left from his smokes of the day before, all carefully dried and collected on the corner of the mantelpiece. He received us in his quietly genial fashion, ordered fresh rashers and eggs, and joined us in a hearty meal. When it was concluded he settled our new acquaintance upon the sofa, placed a pillow beneath his head, and laid a glass of brandy and water within his reach.

"It is easy to see that your experience has been no common one, Mr Hatherley," said he. "Pray, lie down there and make yourself absolutely at home. Tell us what you can, but stop when you are tired and keep up your strength with a little stimulant."

"Thank you," said my patient. "but I have felt another man since the doctor bandaged me, and I think that your breakfast has completed the cure. I shall take up as little of your valuable time as possible, so I shall start at once upon my peculiar experiences."

Holmes sat in his big armchair with the weary, heavy-lidded expression which veiled his keen and eager nature, while I sat opposite to him, and we listened in silence to the strange story which our visitor detailed to us.

"You must know," said he, "that I am an orphan and a bachelor, residing alone in lodgings in London. By profession I am a hydraulic engineer, and I have had considerable experience of my work during the seven years that I was apprenticed to Venner & Matheson, the well-known firm, of Greenwich. Two years ago, having served my time, and having also come into a fair sum of money through my poor father's death, I determined to start in business for myself and took professional chambers in Victoria Street.

"I suppose that everyone finds his first independent start in business a dreary experience. To me it has been exceptionally so. During two years I have had three consultations and one small job, and that is absolutely all that my profession has brought me. My gross takings amount to 27 pounds 10s. Every day, from nine in the morning until four in the afternoon, I waited in my little den, until at last my heart began to sink, and I came to believe that I should never have any practice at all.

"Yesterday, however, just as I was thinking of leaving the office, my clerk entered to say there was a gentleman waiting who wished to see me upon business. He brought up a card, too, with the name of 'Colonel Lysander Stark' engraved upon it. Close at his heels came the colonel himself, a man rather over the middle size, but of an exceeding thinness. I do not think that I have ever seen so thin a man. His whole face sharpened away into nose and chin, and the skin of his cheeks was drawn quite tense over his outstanding bones. Yet this emaciation seemed to be his natural habit, and due to no disease, for his eye was bright, his step brisk, and his bearing assured. He was plainly but neatly dressed, and his age, I should judge, would be nearer forty than thirty.

"'Mr. Hatherley?' said he, with something of a German accent. 'You have been recommended to me, Mr. Hatherley, as being a man who is not only proficient in his profession but is also discreet and capable of preserving a secret.'

"I bowed, feeling as flattered as any young man would at such an address. 'May I ask who it was who gave me so good a character?'

"'Well, perhaps it is better that I should not tell you that just at this moment. I have it from the same source that you are both an orphan and a bachelor and are residing alone in London.'

"'That is quite correct,' I answered; 'but you will excuse me if I say that I cannot see how all this bears upon my professional qualifications. I understand that it was on a professional matter that you wished to speak to me?'

"'Undoubtedly so. But you will find that all I say is really to the point. I have a professional commission for you, but absolute secrecy is quite essential—absolute secrecy, you understand, and of course we may expect that more from a man who is alone than from one who lives in the bosom of his family.'

"'If I promise to keep a secret,' said I, 'you may absolutely depend upon my doing so.'

"He looked very hard at me as I spoke, and it seemed to me that I had never seen so suspicious and questioning an eye.

"'Do you promise, then?' said he at last.

"'Yes, I promise.'

"'Absolute and complete silence before, during, and after? No reference to the matter at all, either in word or writing?'

"'I have already given you my word.'

"'Very good.' He suddenly sprang up, and darting like lightning across the room he flung open the door. The passage outside was empty.

"'That's all right,' said he, coming back. 'I know that clerks are sometimes curious as to their master's affairs. Now we can talk in safety.' He drew up his chair very close to mine and began to stare at me again with the same questioning and thoughtful look.

"A feeling of repulsion, and of something akin to fear had begun to rise within me at the strange antics of this fleshless man. Even my dread of losing a client could not restrain me from showing my impatience.

"'I beg that you will state your business, sir,' said I; 'My time is of value.' Heaven forgive me for that last sentence, but the words came to my lips.

"'How would fifty guineas for a night's work suit you?' he asked.

"'Most admirably.'

"'I say a night's work, but an hour's would be nearer the mark. I simply want your opinion about a hydraulic stamping machine which has got out of gear. If you show us what is wrong we shall soon set it right ourselves. What do you think of such a commission as that?'

"'The work appears to be light and the pay munificent.'

"'Precisely so. We shall want you to come to-night by the last train.'

"'Where to?'

"'To Eyford, in Berkshire. It is a little place near the borders of Oxfordshire, and within seven miles of Reading. There is a train from Paddington which would bring you there at about 11:15.'

"'Very good.'

"'I shall come down in a carriage to meet you.'

"'There is a drive, then?'

"'Yes, our little place is quite out in the country. It is a good seven miles from Eyford Station.'

"'Then we can hardly get there before midnight. I suppose there would be no chance of a train back. I should be compelled to stop the night.'

"'Yes, we could easily give you a shake-down.'

"'That is very awkward. Could I not come at some more convenient hour?'

"'We have judged it best that you should come late. It is to recompense you for any inconvenience that we are paying to you, a young and unknown man, a fee which would buy an opinion from the very heads of your profession. Still, of course, if you would like to draw out of the business, there is plenty of time to do so.'

"I thought of the fifty guineas, and of how very useful they would be to me. 'Not at all,' said I, 'I shall be very happy to accommodate myself to your wishes. I should like, however, to understand a little more clearly what it is that you wish me to do.'

"'Quite so. It is very natural that the pledge of secrecy which we have exacted from you should have aroused your curiosity. I have no wish to commit you to anything without your having it all laid before you. I suppose that we are absolutely safe from eavesdroppers?'

"'Entirely.'

"'Then the matter stands thus. You are probably aware that fuller's-earth is a valuable product, and that it is only found in one or two places in England?'

"'I have heard so.'

"'Some little time ago I bought a small place—a very small place—within ten miles of Reading. I was fortunate enough to discover that there was a deposit of fuller's-earth in one of my fields. On examining it, however, I found that this deposit was a comparatively small one, and that it formed a link between two very much larger ones upon the right and left—both of them, however, in the grounds of my neighbors. These good people were absolutely ignorant that their land contained that which was quite as valuable as a gold-mine. Naturally, it was to my interest to buy their land before they discovered its true value, but unfortunately I had no capital by which I could do this. I took a few of my friends into the secret, however, and they suggested that we should quietly and secretly work our own little deposit and that in this way we should earn the money which would enable us to buy the neighboring fields. This we have now been doing for some time, and in order to help us in our operations we erected a hydraulic press. This press, as I have already explained, has got out of order, and we wish your advice upon the subject. We guard our secret very jealously, however, and if it once became known that we had hydraulic engineers coming to our little house, it would soon rouse inquiry, and then, if the facts came out, it would be good-bye to any chance of getting these fields and carrying out our plans. That is why I have made you promise me that you will not tell a human being that you are going to Eyford to-night. I hope that I make it all plain?'

"'I quite follow you,' said I. 'The only point which I could not quite understand was what use you could make of a hydraulic press in excavating fuller's-earth, which, as I understand, is dug out like gravel from a pit.'

"'Ah!' said he carelessly, 'we have our own process. We compress the earth into bricks, so as to remove them without revealing what they are. But that is a mere detail. I have taken you fully into my confidence now, Mr. Hatherley, and I have shown you how I trust you.' He rose as he spoke. 'I shall expect you, then, at Eyford at 11:15.'

"'I shall certainly be there.'

"'And not a word to a soul.' He looked at me with a last long, questioning gaze, and then, pressing my hand in a cold, dank grasp, he hurried from the room.

"Well, when I came to think it all over in cool blood I was very much astonished, as you may both think, at this sudden commission which had been intrusted to me. On the one hand, of course, I was glad, for the fee was at least tenfold what I should have asked had I set a price upon my own services, and it was possible that this order might lead to other ones. On the other hand, the face and manner of my patron had made an unpleasant impression upon me, and I could not think that his explanation of the fuller's-earth was sufficient to explain the necessity for my coming at midnight, and his extreme anxiety lest I should tell anyone of my errand. However, I threw all fears to the winds, ate a hearty supper, drove to Paddington, and started off, having obeyed to the letter the injunction as to holding my tongue.

"At Reading I had to change not only my carriage but my station. However, I was in time for the last train to Eyford, and I reached the little dim-lit station after eleven o'clock. I was the only passenger who got out there, and there was no one upon the platform save a single sleepy porter with a lantern. As I passed out through the wicket gate, however, I found my acquaintance of the morning waiting in the shadow upon the other side. Without a word he grasped my arm and hurried me into a carriage, the door of which was standing open. He drew up the windows on either side, tapped on the wood-work, and away we went as fast as the horse could go."

"One horse?" interjected Holmes.

"Yes, only one."

"Did you observe the colour?"

"Yes, I saw it by the side-lights when I was stepping into the carriage. It was a chestnut."

"Tired-looking or fresh?"

"Oh, fresh and glossy."

"Thank you. I am sorry to have interrupted you. Pray continue your most interesting statement."

"Away we went then, and we drove for at least an hour. Colonel Lysander Stark had said that it was only seven miles, but I should think, from the rate that we seemed to go, and from the time that we took, that it must have been nearer twelve. He sat at my side in silence all the time, and I was aware, more than once when I glanced in his direction, that he was looking at me with great intensity. The country roads seem to be not very good in that part of the world, for we lurched and jolted terribly. I tried to look out of the windows to see something of where we were, but they were made of frosted glass, and I could make out nothing save the occasional bright blur of a passing light. Now and then I hazarded some remark to break the monotony of the journey, but the colonel answered only in monosyllables, and the conversation soon flagged. At last, however, the bumping of the road was exchanged for the crisp smoothness of a gravel-drive, and the carriage came to a stand. Colonel Lysander Stark sprang out, and, as I followed after him, pulled me swiftly into a porch which gaped in front of us. We stepped, as it were, right out of the carriage and into the hall, so that I failed to catch the most fleeting glance of the front of the house. The instant that I had crossed the threshold the door slammed heavily behind us, and I heard faintly the rattle of the wheels as the carriage drove away.

"It was pitch dark inside the house, and the colonel fumbled about looking for matches and muttering under his breath. Suddenly a door opened at the other end of the passage, and a long, golden bar of light shot out in our direction. It grew broader, and a woman appeared with a lamp in her hand, which she held above her head, pushing her face forward and peering at us. I could see that she was pretty, and from the gloss with which the light shone upon her dark dress I knew that it was a rich material. She spoke a few words in a foreign tongue in a tone as though asking a question, and when my companion answered in a gruff monosyllable she gave such a start that the lamp nearly fell from her hand. Colonel Stark went up to her, whispered something in her ear, and then, pushing her back into the room from whence she had come, he walked towards me again with the lamp in his hand.

"'Perhaps you will have the kindness to wait in this room for a few minutes,' said he, throwing open another door. It was a quiet, little, plainly furnished room, with a round table in the center, on which several German books were scattered. Colonel Stark laid down the lamp on the top of a harmonium beside the door. 'I shall not keep you waiting an instant,' said he, and vanished into the darkness.

"I glanced at the books upon the table, and in spite of my ignorance of German I could see that two of them were treatises on science, the others being volumes of poetry. Then I walked across to the window, hoping that I might catch some glimpse of the country-side, but an oak shutter, heavily barred, was folded across it. It was a wonderfully silent house. There was an old clock ticking loudly somewhere in the passage, but otherwise everything was deadly still. A vague feeling of uneasiness began to steal over me. Who were these German people, and what were they doing living in this strange, out-of-the-way place? And where was the place? I was ten miles or so from Eyford, that was all I knew, but whether north, south, east, or west I had no idea. For that matter, Reading, and possibly other large towns, were within that radius, so the place might not be so secluded, after all. Yet it was quite certain, from the absolute stillness, that we were in the country. I paced up and down the room, humming a tune under my breath to keep up my spirits and feeling that I was thoroughly earning my fifty-guinea fee.

"Suddenly, without any preliminary sound in the midst of the utter stillness, the door of my room swung slowly open. The woman was standing in the aperture, the darkness of the hall behind her, the yellow light from my lamp beating upon her eager and beautiful face. I could see at a glance that she was sick with fear, and the sight sent a chill to my own heart. She held up one shaking finger to warn me to be silent, and she shot a few whispered words of broken English at me, her eyes glancing back, like those of a frightened horse, into the gloom behind her.

"'I would go,' said she, trying hard, as it seemed to me, to speak calmly; 'I would go. I should not stay here. There is no good for you to do.'

"'But, madam,' said I, 'I have not yet done what I came for. I cannot possibly leave until I have seen the machine.'

"'It is not worth your while to wait,' she went on. 'You can pass through the door; no one hinders.' And then, seeing that I smiled and shook my head, she suddenly threw aside her constraint and made a step forward, with her hands wrung together. 'For the love of Heaven!' she whispered, 'get away from here before it is too late!'

"But I am somewhat headstrong by nature, and the more ready to engage in an affair when there is some obstacle in the way. I thought of my fifty-guinea fee, of my wearisome journey, and of the unpleasant night which seemed to be before me. Was it all to go for nothing? Why should I slink away without having carried out my commission, and without the payment which was my due? This woman might, for all I knew, be a monomaniac. With a stout bearing, therefore, though her manner had shaken me more than I cared to confess, I still shook my head and declared my intention of remaining where I was. She was about to renew her entreaties when a door slammed overhead, and the sound of several footsteps was heard upon the stairs. She listened for an instant, threw up her hands with a despairing gesture, and vanished as suddenly and as noiselessly as she had come.

"The newcomers were Colonel Lysander Stark and a short thick man with a chinchilla beard growing out of the creases of his double chin, who was introduced to me as Mr. Ferguson.

"'This is my secretary and manager,' said the colonel. 'By the way, I was under the impression that I left this door shut just now. I fear that you have felt the draught.'

"'On the contrary,' said I, 'I opened the door myself because I felt the room to be a little close.'

"He shot one of his suspicious looks at me. 'Perhaps we had better proceed to business, then,' said he. 'Mr. Ferguson and I will take you up to see the machine.'

"'I had better put my hat on, I suppose.'

"'Oh, no, it is in the house.'

"'What, you dig fuller's-earth in the house?'

"'No, no. This is only where we compress it. But never mind that. All we wish you to do is to examine the machine and to let us know what is wrong with it.'

"We went upstairs together, the colonel first with the lamp, the fat manager and I behind him. It was a labyrinth of an old house, with corridors, passages, narrow winding staircases, and little low doors, the thresholds of which were hollowed out by the generations who had crossed them. There were no carpets and no signs of any furniture above the ground floor, while the plaster was peeling off the walls, and the damp was breaking through in green, unhealthy blotches. I tried to put on as unconcerned an air as possible, but I had not forgotten the warnings of the lady, even though I disregarded them, and I kept a keen eye upon my two companions. Ferguson appeared to be a morose and silent man, but I could see from the little that he said that he was at least a fellow-countryman.

"Colonel Lysander Stark stopped at last before a low door, which he unlocked. Within was a small, square room, in which the three of us could hardly get at one time. Ferguson remained outside, and the colonel ushered me in.

"'We are now,' said he, 'actually within the hydraulic press, and it would be a particularly unpleasant thing for us if anyone were to turn it on. The ceiling of this small chamber is really the end of the descending piston, and it comes down with the force of many tons upon this metal floor. There are small lateral columns of water outside which receive the force, and which transmit and multiply it in the manner which is familiar to you. The machine goes readily enough, but there is some stiffness in the working of it, and it has lost a little of its force. Perhaps you will have the goodness to look it over and to show us how we can set it right.'

"I took the lamp from him, and I examined the machine very thoroughly. It was indeed a gigantic one, and capable of exercising enormous pressure. When I passed outside, however, and pressed down the levers which controlled it, I knew at once by the whishing sound that there was a slight leakage, which allowed a regurgitation of water through one of the side cylinders. An examination showed that one of the india-rubber bands which was round the head of a driving-rod had shrunk so as not quite to fill the socket along which it worked. This was clearly the cause of the loss of power, and I pointed it out to my companions, who followed my remarks very carefully and asked several practical questions as to how they should proceed to set it right. When I had made it clear to them, I returned to the main chamber of the machine and took a good look at it to satisfy my own curiosity. It was obvious at a glance that the story of the fuller's-earth was the merest fabrication, for it would be absurd to suppose that so powerful an engine could be designed for so inadequate a purpose. The walls were of wood, but the floor consisted of a large iron trough, and when I came to examine it I could see a crust of metallic deposit all over it. I had stooped and was scraping at this to see exactly what it was when I heard a muttered exclamation in German and saw the cadaverous face of the colonel looking down at me.

"'What are you doing there?' he asked.

"I felt angry at having been tricked by so elaborate a story as that which he had told me. 'I was admiring your fuller's-earth,' said I; 'I think that I should be better able to advise you as to your machine if I knew what the exact purpose was for which it was used.'

"The instant that I uttered the words I regretted the rashness of my speech. His face set hard, and a baleful light sprang up in his grey eyes.

"'Very well,' said he, 'you shall know all about the machine.' He took a step backward, slammed the little door, and turned the key in the lock. I rushed towards it and pulled at the handle, but it was quite secure, and did not give in the least to my kicks and shoves. 'Hullo!' I yelled. 'Hullo! Colonel! Let me out!'

"And then suddenly in the silence I heard a sound which sent my heart into my mouth. It was the clank of the levers and the swish of the leaking cylinder. He had set the engine at work. The lamp still stood upon the floor where I had placed it when examining the trough. By its light I saw that the black ceiling was coming down upon me, slowly, jerkily, but, as none knew better than myself, with a force which must within a minute grind me to a shapeless pulp. I threw myself, screaming, against the door, and dragged with my nails at the lock. I implored the colonel to let me out, but the remorseless clanking of the levers drowned my cries. The ceiling was only a foot or two above my head, and with my hand upraised I could feel its hard, rough surface. Then it flashed through my mind that the pain of my death would depend very much upon the position in which I met it. If I lay on my face the weight would come upon my spine, and I shuddered to think of that dreadful snap. Easier the other way, perhaps; and yet, had I the nerve to lie and look up at that deadly black shadow wavering down upon me? Already I was unable to stand erect, when my eye caught something which brought a gush of hope back to my heart.

"I have said that though the floor and ceiling were of iron, the walls were of wood. As I gave a last hurried glance around, I saw a thin line of yellow light between two of the boards, which broadened and broadened as a small panel was pushed backward. For an instant I could hardly believe that here was indeed a door which led away from death.

The next instant I threw myself through, and lay half-fainting upon the other side. The panel had closed again behind me, but the crash of the lamp, and a few moments afterwards the clang of the two slabs of metal, told me how narrow had been my escape.

"I was recalled to myself by a frantic plucking at my wrist, and I found myself lying upon the stone floor of a narrow corridor, while a woman bent over me and tugged at me with her left hand, while she held a candle in her right. It was the same good friend whose warning I had so foolishly rejected.

"'Come! come!' she cried breathlessly. 'They will be here in a moment. They will see that you are not there. Oh, do not waste the so-precious time, but come!'

"This time, at least, I did not scorn her advice. I staggered to my feet and ran with her along the corridor and down a winding stair. The latter led to another broad passage, and just as we reached it we heard the sound of running feet and the shouting of two voices, one answering the other from the floor on which we were and from the one beneath. My guide stopped and looked about her like one who is at her wit's end. Then she threw open a door which led into a bedroom, through the window of which the moon was shining brightly.

"'It is your only chance,' said she. 'It is high, but it may be that you can jump it.'

"As she spoke a light sprang into view at the further end of the passage, and I saw the lean figure of Colonel Lysander Stark rushing forward with a lantern in one hand and a weapon like a butcher's cleaver in the other. I rushed across the bedroom, flung open the window, and looked out. How quiet and sweet and wholesome the garden looked in the moonlight, and it could not be more than thirty feet down. I clambered out upon the sill, but I hesitated to jump until I should have heard what passed between my savior and the ruffian who pursued me. If she were ill-used, then at any risks I was determined to go back to her assistance. The thought had hardly flashed through my mind before he was at the door, pushing his way past her; but she threw her arms round him and tried to hold him back.

"'Fritz! Fritz!' she cried in English, 'remember your promise after the last time. You said it should not be again. He will be silent! Oh, he will be silent!'

"'You are mad, Elise!' he shouted, struggling to break away from her. 'You will be the ruin of us. He has seen too much. Let me pass, I say!' He dashed her to one side, and, rushing to the window, cut at me with his heavy weapon. I had let myself go, and was hanging by the hands to the sill, when his blow fell. I was conscious of a dull pain, my grip loosened, and I fell into the garden below.

"I was shaken but not hurt by the fall; so I picked myself up and rushed off among the bushes as hard as I could run, for I understood that I was far from being out of danger yet. Suddenly, however, as I ran, a deadly dizziness and sickness came over me. I glanced down at my hand, which was throbbing painfully, and then, for the first time, saw that my thumb had been cut off and that the blood was pouring from my wound. I endeavored to tie my handkerchief round it, but there came a sudden buzzing in my ears, and next moment I fell in a dead faint among the rose-bushes.

"How long I remained unconscious I cannot tell. It must have been a very long time, for the moon had sunk, and a bright morning was breaking when I came to myself. My clothes were all sodden with dew, and my coat-sleeve was drenched with blood from my wounded thumb. The smarting of it recalled in an instant all the particulars of my night's adventure, and I sprang to my feet with the feeling that I might hardly yet be safe from my pursuers. But to my astonishment, when I came to look round me, neither house nor garden were to be seen. I had been lying in an angle of the hedge close by the highroad, and just a little lower down was a long building, which proved, upon my approaching it, to be the very station at which I had arrived upon the previous night. Were it not for the ugly wound upon my hand, all that had passed during those dreadful hours might have been an evil dream.

"Half dazed, I went into the station and asked about the morning train. There would be one to Reading in less than an hour. The same porter was on duty, I found, as had been there when I arrived. I inquired of him whether he had ever heard of Colonel Lysander Stark. The name was strange to him. Had he observed a carriage the night before waiting for me? No, he had not. Was there a police-station anywhere near? There was one about three miles off.

"It was too far for me to go, weak and ill as I was. I determined to wait until I got back to town before telling my story to the police. It was a little past six when I arrived, so I went first to have my wound dressed, and then the doctor was kind enough to bring me along here. I put the case into your hands and shall do exactly what you advise."

We both sat in silence for some little time after listening to this extraordinary narrative. Then Sherlock Holmes pulled down from the shelf one of the ponderous commonplace books in which he placed his cuttings.

"Here is an advertisement which will interest you," said he. "It appeared in all the papers about a year ago. Listen to this: 'lost, on the 9th inst., Mr. Jeremiah Hayling, aged twenty-six, a hydraulic engineer. Left his lodgings at ten o'clock at night, and has not been heard of since. Was dressed in,' etc., etc. Ha! That represents the last time that the colonel needed to have his machine overhauled, I fancy."

"Good heavens!" cried my patient. "Then that explains what the girl said."

"Undoubtedly. It is quite clear that the colonel was a cool and desperate man, who was absolutely determined that nothing should stand in the way of his little game, like those out-and-out pirates who will leave no survivor from a captured ship. Well, every moment now is precious, so if you feel equal to it we shall go down to Scotland Yard at once as a preliminary to starting for Eyford."

Some three hours or so afterwards we were all in the train together, bound from Reading to the little Berkshire village. There were Sherlock Holmes, the hydraulic engineer, Inspector Bradstreet, of Scotland Yard, a plain-clothes man, and myself.

Bradstreet had spread an ordnance map of the county out upon the seat and was busy with his compasses drawing a circle with Eyford for its center.

"There you are," said he. "That circle is drawn at a radius of ten miles from the village. The place we want must be somewhere near that line. You said ten miles, I think, sir."

"It was an hour's good drive."

"And you think that they brought you back all that way when you were unconscious?"

"They must have done so. I have a confused memory, too, of having been lifted and conveyed somewhere."

"What I cannot understand," said I, "is why they should have spared you when they found you lying fainting in the garden. Perhaps the villain was softened by the woman's entreaties."

"I hardly think that likely. I never saw a more inexorable face in my life."

"Oh, we shall soon clear up all that," said Bradstreet. "Well, I have drawn my circle, and I only wish I knew at what point upon it the folk that we are in search of are to be found."

"I think I could lay my finger on it," said Holmes quietly.

"Really, now!" cried the inspector, "you have formed your opinion! Come, now, we shall see who agrees with you. I say it is south, for the country is more deserted there."

"And I say east," said my patient.

"I am for west," remarked the plain-clothes man. "There are several quiet little villages up there."

"And I am for north," said I, "because there are no hills there, and our friend says that he did not notice the carriage go up any."

"Come," cried the inspector, laughing; "it's a very pretty diversity of opinion. We have boxed the compass among us. Who do you give your casting vote to?"

"You are all wrong."

"But we can't all be."

"Oh, yes, you can. This is my point." He placed his finger in the center of the circle.

"This is where we shall find them."

"But the twelve-mile drive?" gasped Hatherley.

"Six out and six back. Nothing simpler. You say yourself that the horse was fresh and glossy when you got in. How could it be that if it had gone twelve miles over heavy roads?"

"Indeed, it is a likely ruse enough," observed Bradstreet thoughtfully. "Of course there can be no doubt as to the nature of this gang."

"None at all," said Holmes. "They are coiners on a large scale, and have used the machine to form the amalgam which has taken the place of silver."

"We have known for some time that a clever gang was at work," said the inspector. "They have been turning out half-crowns by the thousand. We even traced them as far as Reading, but could get no farther, for they had covered their traces in a way that showed that they were very old hands. But now, thanks to this lucky chance, I think that we have got them right enough."

But the inspector was mistaken, for those criminals were not destined to fall into the hands of justice. As we rolled into Eyford Station we saw a gigantic column of smoke which streamed up from behind a small clump of trees in the neighborhood and hung like an immense ostrich feather over the landscape.

"A house on fire?" asked Bradstreet as the train steamed off again on its way.

"Yes, sir!" said the station-master.

"When did it break out?"

"I hear that it was during the night, sir, but it has got worse, and the whole place is in a blaze."

"Whose house is it?"

"Dr. Becher's."

"Tell me," broke in the engineer, "is Dr. Becher a German, very thin, with a long, sharp nose?"

The station-master laughed heartily. "No, sir, Dr. Becher is an Englishman, and there isn't a man in the parish who has a better-lined waistcoat. But he has a gentleman staying with him, a patient, as I understand, who is a foreigner, and he looks as if a little good Berkshire beef would do him no harm."

The station-master had not finished his speech before we were all hastening in the direction of the fire. The road topped a low hill, and there was a great widespread whitewashed building in front of us, spouting fire at every chink and window, while in the garden in front three fire-engines were vainly striving to keep the flames under.

"That's it!" cried Hatherley, in intense excitement. "There is the gravel-drive, and there are the rose-bushes where I lay. That second window is the one that I jumped from."

"Well, at least," said Holmes, "you have had your revenge upon them. There can be no question that it was your oil-lamp which, when it was crushed in the press, set fire to the wooden walls, though no doubt they were too excited in the chase after you to observe it at the time. Now keep your eyes open in this crowd for your friends of last night, though I very much fear that they are a good hundred miles off by now."

And Holmes's fears came to be realized, for from that day to this no word has ever been heard either of the beautiful woman, the sinister German, or the morose Englishman. Early that morning a peasant had met a cart containing several people and some very bulky boxes driving rapidly in the direction of Reading, but there all traces of the fugitives disappeared, and even Holmes's ingenuity failed ever to discover the least clue as to their whereabouts.

The firemen had been much perturbed at the strange arrangements which they had found within, and still more so by discovering a newly severed human thumb upon a window-sill of the second floor. About sunset, however, their efforts were at last successful, and they subdued the flames, but not before the roof had fallen in, and the whole place been reduced to such absolute ruin that, save some twisted cylinders and iron piping, not a trace remained of the machinery which had cost our unfortunate acquaintance so dearly. Large masses of nickel and of tin were discovered stored in an out-house, but no coins were to be found, which may have explained the presence of those bulky boxes which have been already referred to.

How our hydraulic engineer had been conveyed from the garden to the spot where he recovered his senses might have remained forever a mystery were it not for the soft mold, which told us a very plain tale. He had evidently been carried down by two persons, one of whom had remarkably small feet and the other unusually large ones. On the whole, it was most probable that the silent Englishman, being less bold or less murderous than his companion, had assisted the woman to bear the unconscious man out of the way of danger.

"Well," said our engineer ruefully as we took our seats to return once more to London, "it has been a pretty business for me! I have lost my thumb and I have lost a fifty-guinea fee, and what have I gained?"

"Experience," said Holmes, laughing. "Indirectly it may be of value, you know; you have only to put it into words to gain the reputation of being excellent company for the remainder of your existence."

www.ingramcontent.com/pod-product-compliance
Lightning Source LLC
Chambersburg PA
CBHW031352170626
46807CB00002B/939